## Praise for Kate Hoffmann's Mighty Quinns

"This truly delightful tale packs in the heat
and a lot of heart at the same time."
—*RT Book Reviews* on *The Mighty Quinns: Dermot*

"This is a fast read that is hard to tear the eyes from.
Once I picked it up I couldn't put it down."
—*Fresh Fiction* on *The Mighty Quinns: Dermot*

"A story that not only pulled me in,
but left me weak in the knees."
—*Seriously Reviewed* on *The Mighty Quinns: Riley*

"Sexy, heartwarming and romantic, this is a story to
settle down with and enjoy—and then reread."
—*RT Book Reviews* on *The Mighty Quinns: Teague*

"Sexy Irish folklore and intrigue
weave throughout this steamy tale."
—*RT Book Reviews* on *The Mighty Quinns: Kellan*

"The only drawback to this story
is that it's far too short!"
—*Fresh Fiction* on *The Mighty Quinns: Kellan*

"Strong, imperfect but lovable characters,
an interesting setting and great sensuality."
—*RT Book Reviews* on *The Mighty Quinns: Brody*

*Blaze*®

Dear Reader,

Authors get ideas for books in the funniest places. I came up with the concept of *The Mighty Quinns: Jack* while talking with a friend. He was telling me about his mother's sudden move from Wisconsin to Arizona—all because of a rekindled romance from forty years ago! I immediately began to question him in earnest. After all, how romantic is that—that childhood sweethearts would find each other again after so many years?

Of course, I needed to make a few alterations, but in the end, that one snippet of conversation was enough to build a story.

This kind of thing can sometimes cause a problem for me, though. Conversations I share with my friends are often filled with long pauses, as I play "what if" in my head. If I find something interesting in a comment, I start an interrogation. And my friends sometimes unexpectedly find themselves in my books.

But I guess that's a risk you take when you become friends with a writer. :)

Best wishes,

Kate Hoffmann

# The Mighty Quinns: Jack

## Kate Hoffmann

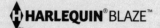

Recycling programs
for this product may
not exist in your area.

ISBN-13: 978-0-373-79750-9

THE MIGHTY QUINNS: JACK

**Printed in U.S.A.**

## ABOUT THE AUTHOR

Kate Hoffmann has written more than seventy books for Harlequin, most of them for the Temptation and Blaze lines. She spent time as a music teacher, a retail assistant buyer and an advertising exec before she settled into a career as a full-time writer. She continues to pursue her interests in music, theater and musical theater, working with local schools in various productions. She lives in southeastern Wisconsin with her cat, Chloe.

Books by Kate Hoffmann

Thanks Paul S.!
This book is for you (and your mom)!

# Prologue

AILEEN QUINN KNELT over the bed of pansies, digging into the soil with her trowel until she'd broken up the clumps around the plants. The wind was chilly and the weather rolling in from the Atlantic was sure to bring rain. But it was spring in Ireland and she was alive to enjoy another summer. At age ninety-six, one couldn't ask for much more.

She braced her hands on the tall handles of her gardening bench and slowly got to her feet. Every day was a blessing, she mused. And with each day came the hope that she would find more members of the family that she'd lost all those years ago.

As one of Ireland's most famous novelists, she lived a charmed life. But it hadn't started that way. She'd been raised in an orphanage, her father killed in the Irish uprising and her mother dead of consumption when Aileen was two. She had spent her life alone, without a single blood relative to call family.

But then, in the midst of doing research for her biography, she learned of her four older brothers—Diarmuid, Conal, Lochlan and Tomas, who had been sent from Ireland by her mother, hoping that her boys would make lives of their own in a more promising place.

Her investigator, Ian Stephens, had already tracked down one descendant, a lovely young man named Logan Quinn who ran a horse-breeding farm outside Brisbane, Australia. He'd also found Logan's parents who had recently visited her in Ireland. She'd given David Quinn and his son, Logan, a sizeable gift from her estate, almost a million dollars each.

Aileen smiled to herself. She had so much money and nothing to do with it. Better that it went to help her family. They were the people who'd be her legacy, the children and grandchildren and great-grandchildren of her lost brothers.

"Miss Quinn?"

Aileen glanced over her shoulder to see Ian Stephens standing at the garden gate. "Hello," she said with a smile. "Either you're early or I've lost all track of time."

"It's half past eleven," he said. "That was when we were supposed to meet, wasn't it?"

She pulled off her gardening gloves and dropped them onto the padded bench. "Yes, it was. Come, let's get out of this dampness and in front of a warm fire. I'm cold to the bone."

Ian offered her his arm as they walked through the garden then onto the wide terrace and into the house. Sally, her housekeeper, appeared almost immediately and helped Aileen out of her jacket. "I've laid a fire in the parlor," she said. "I'll bring you tea."

"Thank you, Sally. And bring a cup for yourself. Mr. Stephens has come with news, haven't you, Mr. Stephens?"

He grinned. "I have. Lots of news. All good."

Aileen nodded. "Then I think we'll also need some of your blackberry scones, as well, Sally. And real butter, not that terrible paste you and Doctor Arnett insist I eat. I'm nearly ninety-seven years old. What harm will a few bites of butter do me now?"

"Yes, ma'am," Sally muttered, sending Ian a secret smile. "But I'm sure Mr. Stephens doesn't keep his trim figure by gobbling down butter every chance he gets."

Ian forced a smile, then cleared his throat. "I'll have butter," he said.

He extended his arm and Aileen slipped her hand into the crook of his elbow. "Let's go find a quiet place to talk, shall we?"

The stone country house was warm and cozy, filled with comfortable furnishings and items she'd collected over a lifetime. They walked to the parlor and Aileen sat down in the chair closest to the fire.

They chatted about the weather until Sally returned with the tea tray. She poured them both a cup and then found a spot for herself on a nearby sofa.

Aileen held out a plate of scones. "Have one. Sally bakes them for me every day. They are the only indulgence left to me, I'm afraid."

As he munched on a scone, Ian opened his portfolio and withdrew a folder, holding it out to her as he wiped his other hand on a linen napkin.

She hesitated before taking it, knowing that the information inside would open yet another door to her past. There were times when the regrets outweighed the joy. "Tell me," she said. "Who have you found?"

"Conal," Ian said, setting his scone down. "And it wasn't a simple task."

She opened the folder to find a copy of a faded photograph. Though she wanted to recognize the face, the subject of the photograph was a stranger. "He's a handsome lad," she said. "I wonder if he resembles my father?"

Ian sat quietly as she studied the photograph. When she looked up at him, he continued. "Conal was hired out as an apprentice to a printer in Cork. Unlike many, this man valued education and Conal attended school until he was sixteen. In his early twenties, he left Cork and started writing for the Irish Independent in Dublin. And when the war broke out in Europe, he covered it. I've copied some of his articles."

"He was a writer? My brother was a writer?"

"Yes, ma'am. And quite a good one from what I could see."

"I used to read that paper," Aileen said. "I might have seen his name." She laughed softly. "If only we might have met. But then, would we have known each other?"

"After the war, he made his way to the U.S. where he settled in Chicago and founded an Irish weekly. He married at age 45 and had two children, a daughter, Mary Katherine, who became a nun, and a son, John, who married in 1975. John had three children, two daughters, Kristina and Katherine, and a son, Jack."

Aileen picked up another photo, turning it over to find the name written on the back. "Jack Quinn."

"He's a sports writer," Ian explained. "And his sisters are both high school teachers."

"And their father?"

"He followed his own father into the news-paper business, but he died of a heart ailment a few years after his youngest daughter was born. From what I've uncovered, the family has struggled, but they are now living comfortably."

"Have you contacted them yet?" Aileen asked.

"Not yet. I'm leaving for Chicago at the end of the week."

Aileen closed the folder and hugged it to her chest. "I'd like to meet them. The whole family. You'll arrange it, won't you? Do all you can to convince them to come?"

"Kristina and Katherine are married and have young children."

"Well, then, I'm looking forward to entertaining little ones. I've never had children in this house. It's about time I did, don't you think?"

"I'll ring you as soon as I've contacted them," Ian said.

He moved to get up but she waved him back into his chair. "You don't have to rush off," she said. "I enjoy your visits."

"I enjoy them, too."

She reached for a photo sitting on the small table next to her chair. "Have I shown you this? Logan sent it to me. He and Sunny got married last month. I was invited to the wedding, but I don't travel much anymore." She stared down at the couple in the photo, Logan dressed in a smart suit and Sunny in a simple flowing dress. They looked so happy, starting out their life together. She handed the picture to Ian.

"They are a lovely couple."

"It's the only regret I've ever had, you know. That I never married and had children." She sighed softly, then put on a bright expression. "I sent them a wedding present. Two handmade Irish riding saddles. They were very pleased. I just got a letter from them last week."

Aileen sat back in her chair and watched as Ian devoured another scone. She was beginning to like this young man. He took his work very seriously, which was a good thing for her. But she worried that he might not have enough time for a personal life. A young man like him ought to be thinking about marriage and a family.

Family was the most important thing in life, she mused. Everyone should have a family to love and treasure. And before the year was over, she hoped to be able to add to the three family members she'd already found, for then, she would be truly rich.

## 1

"This is crazy," Jack Quinn muttered. "I should never have taught you how to use Facebook." He glanced over at his mother, standing quietly next to him in the baggage claim area at the San Francisco airport.

For a woman who had worked so tirelessly her whole life, Elyse Quinn looked remarkably young. But then, he'd noticed a change in her entire demeanor these past few months. He caught her smiling for no reason and the weight of the world seemed to have lifted from her shoulders. She looked…optimistic.

Jack's mother had retired from her teaching job and was now happily looking forward to the next phase of her life. And part of that shift had included more travel. Strangely, her first post-retirement trip wasn't to Europe or Asia, it was to visit an old childhood friend on the West Coast.

Elyse Quinn and Ben McMahon had spent summers as neighbors, their families living in lake cabins next door to each other. But when financial problems caused Elise's family to sell the cabin when she was fourteen, they lost touch with the McMahons. Until Elyse discovered Ben on Facebook and they reconnected.

"Where are we supposed to meet him?" Jack asked, his gaze returning to the baggage carousel.

"Ben said he'd be here to pick us up. I expect if he doesn't find us here, he'll be waiting outside." Elyse glanced over at him. "You really didn't have to come along with me, Jack. I'm perfectly able to travel on my own. I went to Norway last year by myself, after all."

"That was a tour. I'll be damned if I'm going to let you fly halfway across this country to meet some man you barely remember. You don't know anything about him."

"Don't be silly. We've been writing to each other for six months. And phoning. And using Facebook. And Skype. And I know you've done your research, too. If there'd been anything bad about him, you wouldn't have allowed me to buy a plane ticket. Ben McMahon is a nice person and once you meet him, you'll see that."

Jack groaned inwardly. "You know what I think? I think you have romantic feelings for him. You just won't admit it."

Elyse smiled. "Don't be silly. We're old friends and that's all. It's a little late for me to be thinking about romance. And it is possible for a man and a woman to be friends." She sighed softly. "Your father was the one great love of my life. I'm not looking for love."

Jack's thoughts flashed back to the night his father died, the night he'd been called to John Quinn's bedside at the hospital.

The virus had taken away so much of his strength, destroying his heart. Jack had known that the end was near. He'd been nine years old and his father told him that he was now the man of the house. It was his job to protect his mother and two younger sisters.

And so he had, taking on the task with such ferocity that his concern sometimes bordered on obsession. His two younger sisters, now married, had every boyfriend strictly vetted until they brought home two men that Jack had finally found worthy to join the family.

Once Katie and Kris were out of the house, Jack had been left with just his mother to watch over. Luckily, his work as a sports writer had kept him in the Chicago area and her career as a kindergarten teacher had kept her busy. But now that she'd retired, everything had changed.

"There it is," Elyse said, pointing to her bag. "Now where is yours?"

Jack continued to watch the carousel. "Did you call to confirm the hotel rooms?" he asked. "I still think we should have rented a car."

"Ben is more familiar with the city than we are. And parking is so expensive, even at the hotel. I'm sure he knows best."

Ben, Ben, Ben. That's all his mother had been talking about for the past six months.

"What did you do with Roger for the weekend?" Elyse asked.

"He's with Melanie," Jack murmured. He and Melanie had broken up last year after a six-year relationship that his family had assumed would result in marriage. They'd shared a condo, an active social life and a mutt named Roger.

"I sure wish you two could work out your problems," Elyse said.

"Mom, don't start. I told you, that's not going to happen. We're just friends."

Her brow arched. "Just friends. I thought men and women couldn't be just friends."

"Very funny," he muttered. "We're happier this way. Besides, I'm pretty sure she's dating someone else."

Elyse's calm expression shifted to one of surprise. "Oh, Jack, I'm sorry. I always thought you two would end up together. You seem so perfect for each other. I love Melanie. Like a daughter."

"I know, Mom. But that's not going to happen." Jack saw his bag and quickly grabbed it. "All right. Let's go see if we can find our ride."

"I want you to be nice," Elyse warned. "This man is my friend and I don't want you criticizing him like you do some of those ball players in your column."

Jack had done a little research on Ben McMahon. And to his dismay, Ben seemed like a stand-up guy. He'd been married for over thirty years when his wife had passed away three years ago. He'd made his money in the computer industry and he had three daughters.

They headed for the doors, but Elyse reached out and touched his arm. "Wait," she said.

"What's wrong? Are you nervous?" Jack asked.

"A little. But I'm excited, too." She glanced over at him, tears swimming in her eyes. "It seems like just yesterday we were swimming together and roasting hot dogs over a campfire. It's like my life just rushed by without me noticing."

Jack felt a lump of emotion fill his throat. He knew how hard it had been for her. After his father had died so many years ago, she'd put every ounce of her energy into providing for the family. There had been no dates, no men, no thought of remarriage. Just a single-minded desire to give her three children everything she possibly could.

But even though she'd denied any notion of romance, Jack knew that the line between friendship and love was very hard to navigate. "You'll be fine," he said, reaching out to give her a hug. "Just be yourself."

"I feel like a silly teenager," she said. "How am I supposed to be myself?"

They headed toward the sliding door that led outside. As they walked through, a slender woman with blond hair tumbled around her face ran into him, her body slamming against his chest.

She wore a black leather jacket and skinny jeans that clung to her long legs. Her hair was styled as if she'd just run her fingers through the waves after she'd crawled out of bed and her sunglasses were perched on the top of her head.

Jack grabbed her arms as she stumbled back and his gaze meet emerald green eyes. "Are you all right?"

"Sorry," she murmured, stepping to the right just as he stepped to the left. They went back and forth a few times before he grabbed her again.

Then, they both froze and in an instant, their eyes locked. Jack felt a strange current running through his body, the warmth of her flesh seeping through the soft leather jacket. His breathing grew shallow and his mind suddenly lost its ability to form words. She was, in a single word, stunning.

He opened his mouth to speak, but he couldn't come up with anything worth saying. Introducing himself seemed a bit nervy. And asking if they might find a quiet spot to be alone was totally out of the question. What should a guy do in a situation like this?

Kiss her. Every instinct in his body urged him forward, but yet Jack knew that he couldn't do that. She was a stranger and he fancied himself a gentleman.

"I—I really need to get inside," she said. "I'm late."

"Oh, right," Jack mumbled. "Sorry. I—I'll just get out of your—"

The moment he moved, she was gone, disappearing through the sliding-glass doors. He stepped back into the terminal to look for her, but she was already lost in the crowd. Somehow, at that moment, he realized he'd just let opportunity pass him by. What was this powerful attraction, to a complete stranger? And why now, of all days?

He was thirty-one years old and happily single, although not necessarily by choice. He'd always thought that he'd know when the right woman came along. But even after six years with Melanie, the spark just wasn't there.

And here he was, nearly bursting into flames over a stranger. He cursed beneath his breath and brushed the image of the beautiful blonde out of his head, then walked back outside.

He found his mother standing at the curb, staring at a black Mercedes sedan. The hazard lights were on, but there was no one behind the wheel. Airport security had just pulled up and was examining the car.

"What's wrong?"

"Ben said he'd pick me up in a black Mercedes sedan," his mother said. She glanced down the long walkway. "I wonder where he went?"

Jack rolled his suitcase over to his mother. "Watch the luggage. Don't talk to strangers. I'll check to see if he's inside."

In truth, Jack was more interested in finding the blonde, but he knew she was probably long gone. He hurried back through the doors, searching the crowd for a guy who looked like the man he'd seen on Ben McMahon's Facebook page. But as he wove through the waiting passengers, he caught sight of a familiar face.

There she was. The goddess, standing in a spot near some uniformed chauffeurs, holding a sign made out of crumpled paper. As he approached, he searched his brain for something to say. Maybe he should just be honest.

"I'd really like to get to know you? Would you be interested in meeting me for a drink?" he murmured to himself. That seemed a little forward. "Hey, it's you again. Sorry for getting in your way. Maybe I can buy you lunch."

He glanced down at her sign. Maybe he should just pretend he was the person she was looking for. Jack stopped short when he saw "QUINN" scrawled across the paper in ballpoint pen.

"I'm Quinn," he murmured. He hurried up to her, then cleared his throat. "Hey, there. I'm Quinn."

She looked at him and rolled her eyes. "Sure you are."

"No, I am," he said.

"I'm here for an older woman named Elyse."

"That's me," Jack said. "I mean, that's my mom. I'm her son. She's waiting outside. Elyse Quinn."

She gave him a suspicious look, as if weighing the truth of his words against their previous encounter. "If this is just some come on, I really don't have the—"

He held out his hand. "Hey, I'm not messing with you. I'm Jack Quinn, Elyse's son."

She took his hand, folding her fingers against his. The moment caused a tiny shock to rock his body. She had the most beautiful fingers and his mind automatically thought of what those hands might do to his body. He'd never realized that chauffeurs could be so sexy.

"I'm Mia McMahon. I'm Ben's daughter."

All his fantasies screeched to a halt and Jack tried to cover his stunned expression. "His daughter?" His mom had told him that Ben had three daughters, but he'd just assumed they'd be married, and living elsewhere. He searched her hand for a ring and found her fingers bare. For some reason, that made him happy.

She smiled warmly. "I'm sorry. My dad sprained his ankle playing tennis this morning. He's hobbling around on crutches. He would have been here, but he can't drive. So he asked me to look for your mother."

"Well, she's waiting outside. Let's go," Jack said, nodding at her.

She gave him a coy smile. "All right." They wove their way back through the crowd and strolled out the door. But as they made their way back to the Mercedes, Mia took off at a run. The security officer was bent over the hood of the Mercedes, slipping a ticket beneath the wiper.

"No!" she cried, grabbing it and holding it out to him. "I'm here. I'm right here. We're leaving."

He held up his hands and shook his head. "Sorry. You can't leave your car unattended.

There's no parking allowed here at all. You can circle and load, but no stopping to wait."

"But I had to—"

"Nothing you say is going to make me rip up that ticket. You can mail the fine in to the address on the back."

Mia shook her head as he walked away. "Great," she shouted. She glanced down at the ticket. "A hundred and ninety-seven dollars? For five minutes?"

Jack walked up and took the ticket from her fingers. "Don't worry. I'll take care of it. It was our fault."

"No!" she cried, grabbing the ticket back. "Don't be silly. It was my fault."

"It was my mother you were picking up," he countered.

Their gazes met again and for a long moment, Jack lost track of where he was and what he was doing. God, she was pretty. He gently took the ticket from her fingers, then cleared his throat. "Maybe we should get in the car," he said.

"Right," she said.

He dragged their luggage to the rear of the vehicle as Mia popped the trunk. And when he'd finished loading it, he circled back to find that his mother and Ben's daughter had made their introductions and Elyse had taken a spot in the backseat. Jack opened the front door and slid into the luxurious interior, taking a spot next to Mia.

She glanced over her shoulder and pulled away from the curb. "Seat belt," she whispered to him.

"Where is Ben?" his mother asked.

"He sprained his ankle playing tennis this morning." Both Jack and Mia answered at the same time and he chuckled softly. He saw a smile twitching at the corners of her mouth and wondered what was going on inside her head.

Was she as attracted as he was? Jack hoped that her duties for the weekend didn't end with a ride to their hotel. He was going to be alone, for the most part. It might be nice to spend some time with a beautiful woman like Mia McMahon.

MIA'S WEEK OFF HAD NOT started out the way she thought it would. She'd planned to spend the afternoon painting the spare bedroom in her small condo in the Mission District and later, joining a group of friends for dinner.

But a frantic call from her older sister had sent her racing out to the family home in Marin County to help her father get to the doctor after a fall on the tennis court. After that, she'd been tasked with the job of picking up her father's "houseguest" from the airport.

"We're staying at the Stafford Hotel on Union Square," Jack explained. "It would probably be best if we checked in first and—"

Mia frowned. "The Stafford? Oh, no. Actually, you're staying with us. My father said I was to drive you back to the house."

"But we have a reservation," Elyse said. "We couldn't possibly impose."

"Oh, it's no imposition. We have a guest cottage. You and your— You and Jack will be very comfortable there. And you'll have your privacy, as well. And with my father's injury, he won't be driving for a few days. It really would be more convenient."

"Well, then," Jack said, grinning. "I guess that's settled."

"No, it isn't," Elyse said.

Mia looked at Jack, then glanced at his mother in the rearview mirror. "Really, the drive back and forth is almost a half hour. Hotels in the city are ridiculously expensive. You're our guests. And it's absolutely no imposition," she repeated.

"Maybe Mia is right, Mom," Jack said. "We wouldn't want to be any trouble. And since you decided we shouldn't rent a car, it would save on cab fare. Besides, we are only staying two days."

A long, uncomfortable silence descended over the interior of the Mercedes and Mia glanced again between Jack and Elyse's reflection in the rearview mirror. "Thank you for the offer," Jack finally said. "We'd be happy to stay in your guest house."

"Great," Mia said. "Then it's decided."

Now there really was a reason to stick around home for the weekend. She wouldn't even need an excuse. It would be the only hospitable thing to do. Mia pointed out the windshield. "We're going to be crossing the Golden Gate Bridge. Is this your first trip to San Francisco?"

Though she'd meant the question for Elyse, Jack seemed anxious to begin a conversation. And Mia wasn't about to object. She couldn't deny that having the man around for a few days might be nice. And she couldn't help but wonder how he felt about their parents' new "relationship."

Mia had learned about her father's Facebook "affair" a few weeks ago, from her oldest sister, but she hadn't had much time to think about it. In truth, she'd didn't *want* to think about it.

Her mother had died three years ago after a long battle with cancer. As the youngest of three daughters and the only one living near home, she'd been there to help out, to be the caretaker and to support her father during those last days.

And after the funeral, she'd stayed with him for nearly a year, helping him cope with living alone. She made her living as a graphic designer and was able to do most of her work from home, but while she was away, she'd given up on having a life of her own. She'd ignored her friends and pushed her own grief aside to make her father's life easier.

And now, without a second thought, Ben McMahon was ready to move on to someone new. Only she wasn't ready for that to happen. Nor were her two older sisters. They hadn't had enough time. A stab of guilt shot through her. Images of a grasping social-climber had filled her head ever since she'd learned of Elyse's existence. But in all honesty, her dad's "friend" seemed really nice. The kind of woman her mother would have liked.

She fought back a surge of tears. There were moments when she could remember her mother with such pure joy. And then, other times, the memories were so painful, they took her breath away. Mia drew a deep breath and focused her thoughts on something else. Painting. Her new project at work. Jack Quinn.

Jack Quinn? She risked a quick glance across the console, catching sight of his profile in the afternoon sun. He was impossibly attractive, the kind of handsome that took a girl's breath away. She couldn't deny her curiosity. After all, a guy who watched after his mother so carefully couldn't be all bad.

As she stared at the road in front of her, she found herself cataloging his features. Dark hair that was just long enough to wave slightly and thick enough that it would feel good between her fingers. Blue eyes that seemed to see right into her soul. A mouth that curled slightly at the corners, even when he wasn't smiling.

A tremor shook her body and she squeezed tighter on the steering wheel until her knuckles turned white. Maybe this was the reason he'd come here. To distract her from protecting her father. Ben McMahon was a tasty target for any single woman, young or old. He'd made millions in the tech market and now, had nowhere to spend it.

"Here we are," she said, pulling into the driveway. She reached out the window and punched in the security code then waited until the gates slid open in front of them.

"Wow," Jack murmured as they approached the sprawling house at the end of the tree-lined driveway. "No wonder you've got gates. Better to keep the riffraff out."

By the time Mia pulled up in front of the house, her father was standing at the front door, his tall frame balanced on a pair of crutches. The moment the car stopped, Elyse hurriedly stepped out and slowly walked toward him, her hands covering her mouth. A smile broke across Ben's face and Mia felt her breath hitch in her throat. He hadn't smiled like that in years.

Mia's eyes filled with tears and she shoved the door open and got out, brushing the dampness from her cheeks before anyone saw. Jack quickly followed, slamming the Mercedes door behind him as he watched the scene unfold. She joined him, leaning back against the car, her arms crossed over her chest.

"Ben McMahon, you haven't changed a bit," Elyse cried, her musical laugh filling the fragrant air.

"Elyse Lovett, you've only gotten more beautiful."

Mia watched as Elyse hugged her father and a few seconds later, Ben led her into the house, leaving Mia to deal with Jack on her own. "Why don't we get the bags and I'll get you settled in the guest house," she murmured.

They pulled the luggage out of the trunk of the Mercedes and walked around to the rear of the spacious home. Though the house didn't qualify as an estate, it was spacious and comfortable and one of the nicest properties in Marin County. Her father's work had made it possible for the family to live without financial worries. But according to her father, Elyse and her three children hadn't been as lucky.

The guest cottage was located behind the

house, set near the pool and the tennis court. As they walked down the path, she heard Jack chuckle softly.

"What?"

"This is your guest house?"

"Is there something wrong?"

"No. It's just that it's bigger than the house I grew up in."

Mia opened the front door and stepped aside to let him pass. She watched as he took in the beautiful interior. Her mother had redecorated both houses about five years ago and Mia had helped her with her choices. The guest cottage had been her favorite and she and her mother had been very proud of how it turned out. Mia had lived in the cottage the year after her mother had died, the space reminding her of the time they'd spent choosing colors and fabrics.

"The bedrooms are back here," she said.

But he didn't follow her. Instead, he stood in the middle of the living room. "Let me ask you a question. How do you feel about this whole thing? This visit."

Mia slowly turned, setting the bag down beside her. "You mean our parents?"

"Don't you find it a little…odd?"

She sighed deeply and smiled. "Yes?" Finally, someone who understood how she felt. "It's not that I don't want my father to be happy.

After everything that's happened, he deserves to find some happiness. But bringing a complete stranger into our family this late in the game just seems so…unnecessary. I know he imagines himself in love with—"

Jack gasped. "In love? Your father is in love with my—"

"Well, he hasn't really said it," she interrupted. "But he's been so excited about this visit." Mia paused. "What about your mother?"

"She says they're just friends. My father was her one and only."

"Well, then, maybe that's the case. I shouldn't have jumped to conclusions. After all, at their age, romance seems a little too much to hope for."

"Right. Those feelings go away once you turn…what? Fifty?"

"Sixty," she said.

"And there's the matter of the distance," Jack said. "My mother lives in Chicago. Your father lives here. They could never carry on a relationship over that distance."

"Absolutely right."

Jack frowned. "Who knows, they might not even enjoy being together this weekend."

"Yeah, maybe they won't even like each other." She met his gaze and saw the doubt there. Mia walked over to the refrigerator and pulled out a bottled water. "Would you like something to drink? Or maybe something to eat?"

"Do you have a beer?"

She pulled one out and handed it to him, then opened a bottle of water for herself and took a long drink. She had to be very clever about this. After all, her father was in a very vulnerable state and Elyse was a beautiful woman. If she had no feelings for him, then everything was fine. But what if she developed feelings for Mia's father, only to crush his heart later.

Mia pushed away from the counter. "Why don't we get out of here and get some dinner? I'm sure our parents don't need us hanging around, hovering."

She watched as he took a long sip of his beer. Even the way he drank beer was sexy, so casual, so masculine. Her breath caught in her throat and for a long moment, she didn't breathe. The thoughts running through her mind were just a little bit preposterous. And yet, she couldn't deny that Jack Quinn's presence here was like a gift.

It had been too long since she'd had a man in her bed. And now, she'd been given the perfect opportunity—he was handsome, sexy, available and he'd go home at the end of the weekend. Why not take advantage while she could?

She took another swallow of the water, but it went down wrong. Mia coughed, putting her hand on her chest. Her eyes began to water and Jack crossed the room and gently patted her back.

"Are you all right?"

His warm hand smoothed over her back and she nodded. But she wasn't okay. Her thoughts focused on his touch. She wanted him to kiss her, but she wasn't sure exactly how to make it seem as if it was his idea. "I—I'm fine," she said, taking another sip of water. "I think we should go."

"Lead on," Jack said.

Mia walked toward the door, but she was sorely tempted to turn around and walk into the bedroom, just to see what he'd do. If she'd thought he'd follow her, Mia might have tried it.

"You have to try the fish tacos," Mia said, jumping out of the Mini Cooper and slamming the door behind her. Jack crawled out of the car and followed her up to the window of the roadside taco stand.

He stared up at the menu, working his way through the extensive list of choices. After finding their parents engrossed in a study of an old picture album, Jack and Mia had hopped into her car and driven toward the coast. They'd pulled off the highway about fifteen minutes later at a small wooden shack with picnic tables gathered around it.

"I've never had a fish taco," Jack said.

"Don't they have them in Chicago?"

"We're kind of hot dog and pizza people there," Jack explained. "Although it's a great city for food, so I'm sure there are plenty of places to go for fish tacos. I've just never had one."

"Well, Manny's is the best," she said. "It's been around forever. My girlfriends and I used to come here when we were in high school, looking to meet boys. Lots of surfers used to hang out here. Blond, tan, smelling like the ocean."

She ordered a basket of four fish tacos and a couple of beers. When the server handed her a tray, she turned and headed toward one of the picnic tables.

The songs had always touted the superiority of California girls, but Jack had never really seen the attraction. But here, beneath the late-afternoon sun, with a warm breeze blowing off the ocean, he couldn't recall ever meeting a woman more captivating than Mia McMahon.

She grabbed a taco from the basket and bit into it. Jack followed suit and when the mix of fish and fresh tomato and avocado and cheese all melded in his mouth, he groaned softly.

"Good, right?"

"Wow. Really not what I expected," he said.

"I know." She grinned. "So tell me why you decided to come to California with your mother.

Don't you have a job? Or are you a professional mama's boy?"

Jack chuckled. "I wasn't completely convinced that your father wasn't some kind of letch just looking for a little action from a sweet and trusting woman, so I decided to come along and check him out personally. And yes, I do have a job. I'm a sports writer. What do you do? Let me guess. You're either a professional houseguest insulter or a roadside restaurant critic?"

"I'm a graphic designer. I have my own studio. We do a lot of work for restaurants and hotels in the Bay area. Menus, signs, point of sale displays. I designed the sign right over there for Manny."

Jack glanced over his shoulder. "The dancing tacos?"

"They're not dancing, they're hitchhiking," she said. "This is a roadside taco stand. They want a ride." Mia frowned. "I guess it does look like they're dancing."

God, she was adorable, Jack mused. Everything she said was endlessly fascinating, even when it didn't make sense. He took another bite. "I've never seen tacos with legs and arms…and faces, but they look good. You're good."

That brought a laugh. "And you're not a very good liar," she countered. "Don't you think this whole thing is kind of strange?"

"Hitchhiking tacos?"

"No, my dad and your mom. It's kind of un-expected."

He drew a deep breath and nodded. "My dad died twenty-two years ago. I was nine. And since then, Mom's never shown the slightest bit of interest in dating. But she and your dad are old friends. Their families used to spend summers together. It's just a chance to revisit the past."

"My father told me, about a year ago, that he could never see himself with another woman. That my mom was his one true love. I believed him."

"They're looking for companionship," Jack said. "Isn't that what people their age want? I can't imagine they're in it for the sex."

She clapped her hands over her ears. "Stop. I don't want to listen to that."

Jack reached out and pulled her hands away. "At one time they were our age," he said. "I'm sure there were times when they felt that kind of gut-deep attraction for someone. You know, when you feel like you can't breathe and your head gets all fuzzy?" He was very familiar with that feeling, since it had happened to him the moment he'd first seen Mia.

She forced a smile. "Yeah, I know." Mia reached for her beer and took a long sip. "So do you really think that all stops at fifty?"

He shook his head. "No. But then, I'm a guy. I can't believe it's ever going to stop. I'd like to think I'll be interested in sex until I'm at least eighty or ninety years old. What about you?"

"I can't imagine my father having thoughts like that," Mia murmured.

"I wouldn't worry about it. My mother is very comfortable in Chicago and your father is comfortable here. When you get to be that age, you just don't turn your life upside down and move away from the only home you've known for the past thirty years."

She finished her taco and nodded. "We shouldn't get ahead of ourselves. But we should be prepared to discourage a romance." Mia sighed softly. "It would just be so awkward. The holidays would be the worst. Having a stranger there, in place of my mother. It wouldn't feel right."

"Who says she'd want to spend the holidays here? She's always spent Christmas in Chicago with our family."

"See, that's what this leads to. It would be a nightmare. I'm glad we agree that there should be no romance. If it looks like it's getting too hot and heavy, we're going to have to step in."

"Now I'm starting to feel like the parent," Jack said.

"It's what happens. My father only dated one

woman in his entire life. He's not ready for romance."

They finished their tacos and beers, then carried their tray back to the window. Jack walked to the driver's side of the car and reached for the door, but Mia suddenly turned around to face him. "But what if there is an attraction?" she murmured, her gaze fixed on his. "And what if they act on it?"

He stared down at her. They were standing so close he could smell the scent of her perfume, could feel the heat from her body. Jack clenched his hands into fists to keep himself from reaching out and touching her. The breeze toyed with a strand of her hair and he imagined how it might feel between his fingers.

"I suppose we'll deal with that when it happens," he said softly.

Jack leaned in slightly, testing, searching for an equal and opposite reaction. Her lips parted slightly and the need to taste her was almost overwhelming. His gaze drifted down to her mouth. But somewhere, in the back of his mind, a tiny voice told him to stop.

Indulging in his own attraction would be a huge risk. Though Mia was beautiful, she could also distract him from his purpose, which was getting his mother back to Chicago, safely and with her heart intact. And yet, even though his instincts told him to back off, Jack couldn't help but wonder what it would feel like to just let go.

He sucked in a sharp breath, then reached around her and opened the car door. "We should probably get going," he murmured.

"Right," she said, avoiding his gaze.

He smiled to himself as he circled the car. This was the last place on earth he would have ever expected to find a woman who tied him up in knots. Had he known he'd meet someone like Mia, he might have decided to stay at home. Though it would be difficult, he was going to have to keep their relationship strictly platonic.

Unless, of course, she convinced him otherwise.

# 2

"WHAT IS SHE LIKE? Is she pretty? Is she putting on the full court press or is she playing it coy?"

Mia sighed, leaning back against the edge of the kitchen counter as she spoke on her cell phone with her sister Danielle. "She seems really nice. And she is pretty in a very natural way. She has beautiful skin."

"Probably had plastic surgery," Dani said.

"I don't think so. I think she's just naturally beautiful. Like Mom." Mia swallowed hard. "To be honest, I think Mom probably would have liked her." She peeked out the back door to watch her father and Jack's mother. They were enjoying cocktails on the rear terrace, caught up in another private conversation between the two of them.

Dani gasped. "What are you saying? Are you saying you like her?"

"No! I barely know her," Mia protested. "I'm just saying that she isn't some evil stepmonster, out to steal all our father's money and make our holidays a living hell. I don't even think she's interested in romance."

"Every single woman is interested in romance. Especially with a rich and somewhat sexy guy."

"Seriously, I'm watching them right now," Mia said. "All they do is talk."

"What else have you found out?"

"Not much. I've been a little preoccupied with other matters."

"What could be more important than this?" Dani cried.

Mia pulled the phone away from her ear and waited for her sister to calm down. Finally, after a few minutes, it seemed safe to proceed. "She brought her son with her. And he's…he's…" Maybe it would be best to just say it out loud. "He's incredibly hot."

"What?"

"Nothing," Mia said. "I—I have to go now."

"He's hot? Who's hot? Mia, what is going on?"

"I've got to run," Mia said. "Call you later." She quickly turned off the phone, then silenced the ringer, as well. No doubt Dani would call

Steph, and then Steph would be on the line in a few minutes demanding answers of her own.

She walked through the kitchen and out into the late-afternoon sun shining on the wide terrace. Only her father and Elyse weren't sitting at the table anymore. "Daddy?"

She walked back inside and called out again. But the house was silent.

They couldn't have gone far. Her father was still hobbling around on crutches. She decided to pay a visit to the guesthouse and grabbed a pitcher of iced tea from the refrigerator to offer as an excuse.

She found Jack sitting on the small patio at the front of the house, his computer open on the teak table in front of him. When he heard her footsteps on the gravel path, he turned and smiled. "Hey, there."

"Hi," Mia said. "I brought you and your mom some iced tea."

"She's not here. I thought she was still with your dad."

Mia set the pitcher down on the table. "No. They're not in the house."

Jack slowly stood. "Where do you think they've gone?"

"Well, they can't be far. My dad can't drive."

"My mother can," he countered.

"I wonder if the car is still here."

They both hurried back down the path and then circled the house to the wide driveway. The black Mercedes was nowhere in sight.

"Great," he muttered. "I thought you were going to keep an eye on them."

"They're not children," Mia snapped. "What was I supposed to do, pull up a chair and watch them every second?"

"No, but you certainly should have known if they decided to go somewhere. Doesn't your father let you know when he leaves the house?"

"No. Does your mother tell you her every move?" Mia replied.

"Yes, she usually does. It's just something we do in our family. We take care of each other." Jack turned to face her. "Where do you think they went?"

"Dinner? We didn't have much in the fridge and I'm sure they were starting to get hungry. They probably went to Serafina's, a restaurant in town. It's one of my dad's favorite places."

"Let's go, then," Jack said, starting toward her car.

"You want to go get them?"

"No, I want to see what they're doing. How are we supposed to keep this under control when we don't know what's going on?"

Mia shook her head. "I'm not spying on them."

"Who says we have to spy? You and I just

decided to go out and get a drink and, funny enough, we just happened to end up at your dad's favorite restaurant."

Mia stared at him for a long moment. "Wow. Do you let your mother go grocery shopping on her own or do you follow her around with the cart telling her what cereal to buy?"

Jack shook his head and held out his hand. "If you don't want to go, give me your keys."

Mia couldn't help but think he was going too far. What could possibly happen between Ben and Elyse when they were out in public? "You know, my dad isn't such a bad guy. In fact, he's really kind of a catch."

"I'm sure he is," Jack said. His expression softened. "I know he is. It's just that my mom hasn't dated at all in more than forty years. If your dad makes some kind of move, she won't know what to do."

"I think you underestimate your mom," Mia said.

Mia got behind the wheel, Jack jumped in the passenger seat and they sped off towards town. When they reached the restaurant, they noticed the black Mercedes parked out front. Mia gave the keys to the valet and she and Jack walked inside and found a spot at the end of the bar. Most of the dining room was visible through a wide arched opening in the wall and after a quick search, Mia located her father and Elyse at a booth within easy sightlines.

Jack ordered them both a glass of wine and they settled onto the comfortable stools. "He's holding her hand," Mia said, craning her neck.

Jack glanced over and cursed beneath his breath. "Already? Your father moves fast."

"Holding hands is fast? Just because a woman holds a guy's hand, it doesn't mean they want to sleep together."

"There's a lot you can communicate through holding hands," Jack insisted.

"Oh, please," Mia said. "Teenagers hold hands. It's…kind of sweet. They're just friends."

Jack grabbed her hand and laced his fingers through hers, gently pinning her arm onto the bar. He slowly slid his fingers back and forth in a lazy rhythm that was startlingly sexual in nature.

Mia swallowed hard and tried to maintain her composure. The feel of his palm pressed against hers, trapping her hand on the cool wood of the bar. Mia's breath caught when he turned her hand over and ran his index finger along a line from her wrist to her forearm.

"Holding hands can lead to all sorts of things," he murmured, his gaze fixed on the spot where he touched. A tiny smile played at the corners of his mouth and Mia realized that he was enjoying this—almost as much as she was.

She swallowed a groan when he flipped her hand over and began to draw lazy circles on her palm. If this was what he did to a woman just holding her hand, what might he do to her in bed? Though Mia wasn't unfamiliar with the seductive powers of the opposite sex, she certainly had never enjoyed the pleasures of a man who really knew what he was doing in the bedroom. She thought those men only existed in movies and erotic novels.

"I—I think you've proved your point." Her voice cracked slightly and she pulled her hand away from him to grab her wineglass.

"Thank you," he said with a self-satisfied smile.

"Although, I really doubt that my father possesses that level of skill at seduction." This time she did allow herself to groan out loud. "I never thought I'd be talking about my father's sex life. This is ridiculous."

"They've had six months of exchanging letters and phone calls," he said. "You have to expect some level of…longing."

A giggle burst from her lips. "Longing? You seem to have an awful lot to say about romance. Are you speaking from experience? Or do you just do a lot of reading?"

"I'm a journalist," he said. "I'm observant."

"How many times have you been in love?"

The moment she asked the question, she wanted to take it back. It was too personal and made her seem too interested in his past. She'd only met him seven hours ago.

"A few," he said. "What about you?"

Mia wasn't sure whether she ought to tell him the truth—that she'd never been in love—or whether it would be better to just lie. "Same," she said.

In truth, she'd never really allowed herself to completely surrender to a man. While her mother was ill, she'd been too preoccupied to think about a social life and after her mom died, Mia spent her spare time with her dad, helping him cope with living on his own.

Maybe it was time to think about herself. What was wrong with indulging in a little romance with Jack Quinn? A kiss here or there might be fun. And she had a feeling that the sex would be incredible. And better still, he'd be gone in a few days, which meant that she wouldn't have to deal with any long-term consequences. Unless, of course, Ben and Elyse ended up together and she had to face Jack at family functions.

Well, there was the perfect reason not to indulge her fantasies about this man. Knowing her sisters, they'd be able to see it the moment he walked into the room. And the last thing she'd want is to be fantasizing about her stepbrother over Thanksgiving dinner. That was just—weird.

"Look, look."

His voice interrupted her thoughts and she looked over at the table to see her father draw Elyse's hand to his lips. Mia held her breath as he kissed it and she felt emotion well up inside her.

Even after three years, she still saw sadness in his eyes. But now, he seemed so happy, so…young and carefree. Was it selfish of her to want him to be alone for the rest of his life? She couldn't imagine that he'd ever be able to replace her mother, but maybe it wasn't about replacing what he'd lost, but finding something completely new.

Tears pushed at the corners of her eyes and she drew in a sharp breath. "We have to go," she said, grabbing her purse from the bar. "Now."

She hurried toward the door, weaving through the patrons waiting for a table. When she reached the sidewalk, she stopped short and gulped in a deep breath of the cool evening air. The parking valet approached her and she held out her hand to stop him, then took off down the sidewalk.

The farther she got away from the restaurant, the less she knew what she was crying about. Was this about her father or was it about her own pathetic love life? For the first time in years, she found herself attracted to a man and she couldn't bring herself to act on it.

Why couldn't she have met Jack Quinn in a bar or at the grocery store? She could have indulged in a quick and simple affair without a second thought.

"Mia! Hey, wait up."

She brushed the tears off her cheeks and pasted a smile on her face, then turned.

When he caught up to her, Jack reached out and gently grabbed her arm. "What's wrong? Are you all right?"

"I'm fine. Just a little overwhelmed, that's all."

He stared down into her eyes. "I'm sorry. I know this is hard for you."

Mia nodded and fought back a fresh surge of tears. She laughed softly. "I really miss my mom."

His hand moved to her cheek and he brushed the dampness away with his thumb. "Don't cry."

"Actually, I think a good cry is exactly what I *do* need," Mia said. She'd kept her emotions in check for so long, trying to stay strong for her father. But now, it felt as if she could finally let go. He was fine now. And she was a mess.

"I'm sorry," he murmured. He stared down into her eyes, searching her gaze. And then, cupping her cheek in his hand, he turned her face up to his and kissed her.

Her breath caught the instant before their lips touched and she felt giddy and light-headed. And then, his mouth covered hers in a deep and delicious kiss. Mia's knees wobbled and she grabbed the front of his shirt to balance herself, her fingers splaying against his chest.

He took her touch as an invitation and the kiss grew more passionate as he molded her mouth to his. Mia knew she'd been kissed before. But she was also certain that she'd never been kissed like this, with such raw desire and unbridled lust.

When he finally drew back, they just stared at each other for a long time, neither one of them sure what to say. "What do you want to do?" he asked.

She wanted to kiss him again. But Mia knew that wasn't what he was asking. "Maybe we should just leave them alone."

Jack nodded. "All right. I think that would be best."

As they walked back to the parking valet, he grabbed her hand and drew it to his lips, pressing a kiss below her wrist. "I'm sorry if I caused those tears."

"Sometimes it feels good to cry," Mia said, drawing a ragged breath. And sometimes, it felt really good to kiss a man.

WHEN THE VALET BROUGHT the car, Mia handed Jack the keys, then crawled in the passenger side, slumping down in the seat and pulling her knees up to her chest.

"Where to?" he asked.

Mia shrugged. "I don't care, just drive."

Jack started the car and pulled out into the street, then wove through the village until he found the highway. The night was warm and the top was still down on the little convertible. April in Chicago could be chilly and damp. If he couldn't enjoy kissing Mia, he'd at least enjoy the weather. He turned south, following the signs for the city.

"Are you all right?" he asked.

Mia nodded. "I just get emotional at times. Whenever I really need my mother, I just feel so…lost. I should go see a shrink. I'm just not dealing with my grief very well."

"Why? Because you miss your mom? Mia, if you want my opinion, you don't want to lose those feelings. It's all right to miss her. I still miss my dad. I still have imaginary conversations in my head with him. We talk about all kinds of things."

"Really?" she said, turned toward him. "I do that, too. Lately, I've been trying to stop myself. I mean, I don't actually think she's here, but I kind of feel like she might be listening."

"Maybe she is. I like to think the same thing about my dad."

They drove for a long time in silence and when they reached the intersection for Highway 1, Mia pointed to the right. "Turn here."

The highway twisted and turned, past residential areas and then leading into thick, dark forests. Jack kept his attention on the road, watching for sudden switchbacks and sharp curves. He suspected they were heading toward the coast and when he spotted signs for Muir Beach, he decided to pull off the road and into a parking lot.

He turned off the car and faced her. She seemed lost in her thoughts and he wasn't sure whether he ought to interrupt. But then she turned to him suddenly. "What do you think of the notion of friends with benefits?"

Jack gasped softly. "Is that what you think is going on with your father and my—"

"No!" She drew a deep breath. "No. I was talking about us." Mia frowned. "You do know what I'm talking about, don't you?"

Jack held up his hand. "Yes. I know exactly what you're talking about." The twist in the conversation was completely unexpected. Hell, he'd been great at handling the hairpin turns on the road, but now, he wasn't quite sure what to say. "Are we friends?"

"More like acquaintances. But I think we could be friends, given a little more time."

"I agree," he said. "So, why do you think this would work?"

Mia drew a deep breath, then reached out and grabbed his hand. She placed it on her chest. "Can you feel that?"

"Your heart?"

She nodded. "Feel how fast it's beating? I can hardly catch my breath sometimes. And my brain is all mixed up." Mia paused. "I haven't felt like this in three years. In fact, I really haven't felt anything in three years. I've made myself numb just to avoid feeling sad. And now, for the first time in a long time, I'm not numb anymore."

He reached out and smoothed his hand over her cheek. "That's good."

Mia nodded. "Yes. And you have to admit, there is an attraction. I mean, I wasn't sure, but then you kissed me. There is an attraction, isn't there?"

"Oh, yes," Jack replied.

"Then we should act on it."

"Right now?"

"Not immediately. But soon. You are going home in a few days."

He watched her face, searching for some clue to her feelings. But it was difficult to see much in the feeble light from the parking lot. "Come on. Let's take a walk."

He jumped out of the car and then circled around to open her door. Jack held out his hand and she placed her fingers in his. "This way," she said. "There's a walk to the overlook."

A light mist hung in the air and Jack pulled her close to him to protect her against the chill in the air. "So, you really think this is going to work?" he asked. "No strings, no expectations?"

"I think it could," she said. She turned to face him, grabbing the front of his shirt. "Kiss me again."

Jack took her face between his hands. He knew it would have to be good, something that would soothe her doubts and insecurities. He bent close and touched his lips to hers. The moment they made contact, he felt his blood turn to fire in his veins.

A tiny sigh slipped from her lips as she wrapped her arms around his neck and he pulled her tight against his body. Every fantasy he'd had about touching her was instantly brought to life. She was warm and soft and Jack smoothed his hands over her hips.

There was no doubt in his mind that they'd be good together. Better than good, he suspected. Jack's mouth molded to hers and the kiss deepened, the taste of her like some exotic nectar. Her body trembled beneath his touch and he drew back. "Are you cold?"

She shook her head. "No." Mia grabbed his hand and drew him along the walkway, the fog growing thicker around them until he could barely see her beside him. He could hear her footsteps, feel her hand in his, but he was almost blind. And then, she stopped.

Jack felt her hands moving over his body and he leaned into her warmth. Without the benefit of sight, his other senses seemed more acute. He could hear every breath she took as well as the sound of his heart beating inside his own chest. In the distance, waves crashed against rocks— or was that the blood rushing through his veins?

Jack pressed her back against the railing and then yanked her hips against his. He was already hard, the need growing more intense with every moment that passed. There wasn't much they could do, standing out on the edge of some invisible cliff. And yet, each caress was impossibly erotic, driving him to the limits of his desire.

He ran his hand beneath her shirt, splaying his fingers against the warm flesh at the small of her back. The longer they stood in the swirling fog, the colder it seemed to get and when he heard her teeth chatter, he picked her up and hugged her body to his.

"Let's go back to the car," he murmured. He

took her hand and they hurried along the walk-way, using the rail to guide them through the dark. When they reached the Mini Cooper, they put the top up and then got inside, Jack behind the wheel. He started the car and turned on the heater, then fiddled with the radio until he found a station with soft jazz music.

"Better?" he asked.

Mia held her hands up to the heat. "Much better," she said. "This is spring in San Francisco."

"We don't drive in fog like this in the mid-west," Jack said, peering out the window.

"Oh, don't worry. It disappears as quickly as it rolls in. Just wait a bit and it will be gone."

"What are we going to do until then?" Jack asked.

"What everyone else does in the fog," she said. Mia twisted in her seat, then crawled over the console, settling herself on Jack's lap. He reached down for the lever on the seat and it slid back.

"Try the other one," she murmured, her body settling against his as she straddled his hips.

He found it and the seat back released until he was nearly lying down beneath her. "That's convenient," he said with a chuckle. "Now what?"

"I think it's time for those benefits," she murmured. Mia reached down for the hem of her shirt. Not bothering with the buttons on the crisp cotton blouse, she pulled it over her head. The lights in the parking lot offered a hazy illumination and he could make out a lacy scrap of a bra in a pale color.

Jack let out a tightly held breath, then reached up to smooth his hand over her breast. A tiny moan slipped from her throat as he rubbed his thumb across her nipple. A few hours ago, he'd been wondering how he might make this happen. And now, it was happening with very little effort at all….

He couldn't help but wonder what was going through her mind. From what he'd been able to glean, she'd never really gotten over her mother's death. Even after three years, she seemed to be… fragile, and vulnerable. Was this really what she wanted or was she, as she admitted, just grasping for something to make her feel anything?

Mia's fingers tangled in his hair and she bent close and kissed him, her tongue teasing at his. She was perfect, he mused. Exactly what he needed at the moment. With a facile touch, he twisted his fingers through her bra strap and drew it down over her shoulder. Jack cupped her warm flesh in his palm, slowly bringing her nipple to a peak through the silky fabric. And when it was hard, Jack leaned forward and pulled the bra aside.

His lips found her nipple and he teased at it

with his tongue. It had been a while since he'd enjoyed any intimacies with a woman. After Melanie, there'd been a few one-night stands, but nothing worth remembering. Yet, here he was, indulging again in no-strings sex. But it didn't feel that way. There was some strange connection between the two of them, as if they weren't really strangers at all.

Mia reached for the buttons of his shirt and worked at them until she reached his lap. She parted the crisp fabric, exposing his naked chest. Then, with a soft sigh, she stretched out on top of him. Suddenly, he felt her stiffen.

"Ow," she said, wincing. "Ow, ow. Cramp."

She tried to roll off of him, but got caught against the gearshift. A curse burst from her lips and when she could move again, she crawled over him and tumbled into the backseat. Stretching her leg above her, she rubbed her calf.

Jack twisted in his seat and watched her. "Maybe we should take this elsewhere?"

She glanced over at him, then began to laugh. "Come back here," Mia said, holding out her hand.

"I'm not sure that's physically possible. This car is better suited for a family of gnomes."

"Oh, but it's so easy to park in the city," she said.

"It is not physically possible for me to occupy the same space as you."

Mia sighed dramatically. "So what are we going to do?" she asked. She reached for her boots and tugged them off her feet, then tossed them on the floor along with her socks.

Jack held his breath as she made her way back to the front seat. Hell, he didn't know what was going to happen next. But he was pretty sure she was ready to enjoy it.

MIA SLIPPED HER FINGERS through his hair and pulled Jack into another kiss, curling up on his lap, her body wedged against the steering wheel. She'd expected to be nervous. After all, it had been almost a year since she'd made love to a man. She couldn't remember much about that night, only that it hadn't been what she was looking for.

But this was different. There was warmth and sweetness here with Jack, an attraction that couldn't be denied. When he touched her, she shivered and burned at the same time, her body aching for more. It would be all right. He would make it all right.

The windows in the car had steamed up and the heat was warm on her bare skin. It was impossible to do much in such a confined space, but that didn't keep Jack from exploring her body. His hand skimmed over her naked skin, tracing a path from her shoulder to her breast and then lower, the caress leaving a warm imprint.

"What do you want?" he whispered, his breath warm against her ear.

"I'm not sure what I want would be possible in this car," she said. "Although it might be fun trying. Maybe I should have bought a Prius. They're much roomier."

His fingers found the button on the front of her jeans. He flipped it open, then slowly drew the zipper down. "Let's see what we can do, shall we?"

Mia smiled as he slid his hand lower, moving toward the moist spot between her legs. She shifted, allowing him to touch her freely against the tight jeans.

It was such an intimate act and she felt completely vulnerable to him, but Mia didn't care. He was taking her exactly where she wanted to go and she didn't want to stop. She felt free and alive, as if the dark cloud hanging over her had suddenly burst into a warm shower.

His mouth found hers, catching her in a deep and powerful kiss. She arched against him and his fingers moved closer. Mia stretched her leg out, pressing her foot against the passenger-side window. It was just enough to bring another cramp in her calf and Mia cried out.

His kiss grew more passionate and Mia realized that he thought she was in the midst of an orgasm. "Cramp," she cried.

"What?" he said, drawing back.

"Another cramp. Ow. Oh, this one is bad. Damn it's in my foot now." She looked down at her bare foot to see her toes curl. A giggle slipped from her lips. He'd made her toes curl.

"Does this always happen when you get… excited?"

Her eyes began to water from the pain and she tried to stretch her leg, but the car was just too small to move. "No. It just happens when I take a 5-mile morning run that's mostly uphill and then forget to stretch in the afternoon." She gasped. "I think I'm going to die here."

Jack opened the door and slid out of the car. A few moments later, he opened the passenger side and sat down, pulling her legs onto his lap. "Which one?"

"Left," she said. "Foot."

He began to massage her foot, kneading the arch with his thumbs, then moving to her ankle and then her calf. The interior of the car was warm and cozy against the chill outside. It was as if they were in their own little world. Nothing existed outside of the two of them.

Mia closed her eyes and leaned back against the door. "That feels so good."

"I always eat bananas," he murmured.

She opened her eyes, laughing. "What?"

"To prevent cramps. I think it's the potassium."

"Electrolytes," she said. "Do you run?"

"Only if someone is chasing me," he said, chuckling. "No, I usually try to get in five miles three or four times a week."

"And what else do you do to get that body?" she asked, pressing her other foot against his naked chest. She wanted—no, needed—to know more about him. Maybe then she'd understand this undeniable attraction. Was this simply physical? Or was there more to it?

"I play a little basketball with the guys at the office."

"Tell me about your office," she said.

He observed her for a long moment, still gently rubbing her foot. "Why the questions?"

"Conversation is about all we have right now. My body is telling me we should slow down a little."

"Your body is telling you this car is too small for any kind of fun," he countered.

Mia paused and watched him. "Usually I know someone a little better before we…you know…"

"Do it?" he asked.

"Yes. It's just a little strange."

"What do you want to know? Ask me anything."

"You said you'd been in love a few times. What about the last time? What was she like?" Usually, Mia wasn't so bold, but this wasn't an ordinary relationship. It was kind of like guerrilla seduction. There were no rules, nothing was out of bounds.

"She's really nice," he said. "We're still friends. We were together for six years."

Mia gasped. "Six years? That's a long time. Why so long?"

"It didn't seem like a long time," Jack said. He glanced up from her foot. "Oh, you're asking why we didn't get married?"

"It's a valid question, don't you think?"

Jack shrugged. "That was my fault. It just never felt like the right time. Or maybe, the right time for me. She wanted to get married. I was ambivalent."

"Why do you think that was?"

He grabbed her foot and pressed a kiss into her instep. "Maybe we should get back to those benefits we were enjoying. You don't want to hear all my sad stories."

"Maybe it was because you didn't want to love someone and lose them again? Like you lost your father?"

"I don't know. That's different. I think it was

because she wasn't the right one. I think when the right one comes along, I'll know it."

"Maybe," she said. She smiled at him. "You made my toes curl. That's a start."

He laughed, then grabbed her hands and pulled her on top of him, wrapping his arm around her. "How's your leg?"

"Better," she said, dropping a kiss on his lips. "It's been quite a day."

Mia snuggled against him. "Very unexpected." She closed her eyes and let her thoughts drift. She felt comfortable in his embrace, completely relaxed...warm...safe.

She didn't realize she was asleep until the chill woke her up. Snuggling closer to his chest, she searched for warmth, but it wasn't enough. Reluctantly, Mia opened her eyes only to find the light of morning filling the car. She sat up straight, then realized that sometime during the night, Jack had turned off the ignition. The car was silent.

She twisted in her seat and wiped the moisture off the window, peering out into the bright morning light. "Time," she murmured. Mia grabbed Jack's wrist, causing him to jerk awake.

"What?" he said, frowning.

"Time," she said, pulling his watch in front of her. Mia swiped at her sleepy eyes then groaned.

"It's almost seven-thirty. We need to get back to the house."

Mia crawled into the driver's seat and started the car. To her relief, there was still enough gas to get home. "How did we fall asleep?" She glanced over at him. He was still half-asleep.

"I don't know. Can we stop for coffee?"

"No! We have to get home."

"Why?"

She drew a deep breath, then took a moment to consider his question. Why? They were virtual strangers. They'd spent the night together. And though they hadn't indulged in a full-scale seduction, they had messed around a little bit. On the other hand, they were both adults.

"Do you want to explain this to my father?" she asked.

"Will he even notice?" Jack countered. He shook his head. "Don't worry. We took a drive. The fog set in. We stopped and then fell asleep." He reached for her shirt and passed it to her. "You may want to put this on. The story will probably be easier for him to swallow if you aren't dressed topless."

Mia glanced over at him. A giggle burst from her lips and she leaned back into the leather seat. This was crazy. Her once orderly and unremarkable life had been turned upside down by the appearance of a handsome man. She was tear-ing off her clothes and kissing in cars and—and feeling more alive than she had in years.

Grudgingly, she took the blouse from his hands and unbuttoned it. "He and your mother probably won't even have noticed we were gone last night," she said.

"Oh, I wouldn't count on that," he said. "My mother notices everything."

"Right. I suppose you have to let her know when you'll be in at night or she'll wait up?"

"Are you under the impression that I live at home?"

She pulled the blouse on and started on the buttons. "I thought you said—"

"No," Jack said. "I don't live with my mother."

"But you—"

"I have a flat in Wicker Park. I live about thirty minutes from where I grew up."

"Oh, well, never mind, then. So she won't be waiting up."

"Maybe not. But she's going to wonder where we were all night. Maybe if you drive fast, we can make it home before she gets up. If we're lucky, they had a very late night last night and they're both sleeping in."

Mia turned on the car, then glanced over at him and smiled. She couldn't help herself. She reached out and grabbed his face and pulled him into a long and very expressive kiss. "Good morning," she said.

Jack chuckled as he shook his head. "Drive. Before you get us in any more trouble."

It was a good morning. Even though she didn't sleep well, she felt as though anything was possible. She felt…optimistic. As if she'd cast off the gloom of the past three years and walked into the sunlight—and right into Jack Quinn's arms.

# 3

WHEN THEY GOT BACK TO the house, Mia and Jack hopped out of the car and went their separate ways, promising to meet up in a half hour for breakfast. Mia had insisted on making a quick stop at a bakery in town, determined to have an excuse for her early absence.

Jack had decided that he'd just take a wait-and-see approach. To his relief, he heard the shower running in his mother's bathroom when he stepped through the front door of the guest cottage. His bedroom door was closed and as soon as he got inside, he stripped off his clothes and redressed, this time in a T-shirt and running shorts. Then he tossed some water on his hair and walked out into the kitchen, determined to make a pot of very black coffee.

As he stood and watched the coffee stream into the glass pot, his mother emerged, wrapped in her favorite robe, her hair damp. "Oh, thank God you're making coffee." She stood next to him and waited, her gaze fixed on the coffee-maker.

"Late night last night? I didn't hear you come in," Jack said.

"Not surprising, since you weren't in yet at four."

"You stayed out until four a.m.?" Jack asked, stunned at his mother's behavior. She'd always been early to bed. Eleven was the latest she stayed up.

"It was wonderful," she said. "We never stopped talking. And I was afraid that we'd talked about everything over the internet these past six months."

Jack thought he saw a blush color her cheeks. "So, it went well?"

"It went really well. And I should be exhausted, but I'm not. Today, we're going to a farmer's market and taking a winery tour. Then we're going to drive into the city, have dinner there and see a movie. *Dr. Zhivago.*"

"That's one of your favorites."

"Ben and I saw the movie the last summer my family spent at the cabin. I've never been able to watch that movie without thinking about him."

She was so excited that her whole demeanor had changed. She wasn't his sixty-three-year-old mother anymore, she was a silly, flustered young woman. And though he wanted to warn her about becoming too invested, too early, Jack just couldn't bring himself to kill her happy mood.

"I'm glad. It's too bad you have such a short time together."

"It is," Elyse said wistfully. "You know, I'm kind of hoping he'll ask me to stay a little longer."

Jack forced a smile. "He'd be a fool not to."

She looked up at him. "You're a good son."

He felt a sliver of guilt. Was he really a good son? If he was, then maybe he might be more enthusiastic about her finding a new man. Maybe he ought to just allow her the chance to try again and stop worrying about a relationship failing.

"Yes, I am," Jack said. He opened the cupboard and reached for a pair of mugs, then filled one for his mother. She gave him a grateful smile and took a sip.

Elyse nodded. "Now, why don't you tell me where you were until just a few minutes ago?"

Jack paused. "I was with Mia."

His mother studied him for a long moment. "I'm not sure I should be happy about that. Are you telling me you spent the night together?"

"In the technical sense. But not in the biblical

sense. We took a drive, it got foggy, we waited for the fog to lift and ended up falling asleep."

"And that's it?" she asked as she smoothed her hands over her coffee mug.

"Yes," he lied. Hell, there were some things that he had to keep private.

"She's a lovely girl," Elyse commented. "You could do a lot worse."

"Mom, I—"

Elyse held out her hand and shook her head. "Just listen to me for a moment. You have spent your whole life watching out for our family. But now it's time for you to put down that burden and start to think of a family of your own. I think that's why things didn't work out with Melanie. We were always more important to you."

"You'll always be—"

"No, we won't. You're going to meet someone and she'll take your breath away. She's the one who will mean the most to you."

Jack swallowed hard. Mia took his breath away. But he'd known her for exactly one day, not long enough to make any lifelong decisions. "Don't get ahead of yourself," he warned.

"Just promise me that you'll start to think more about yourself," she murmured. "I can survive quite nicely on my own. And your sisters will be fine, too."

Jack stared at her for a long moment. He wasn't sure he understood what she was saying.

"I know about the job offer in Los Angeles," she continued. "And I think you should consider it."

"How did you find out?"

"I called your office a few weeks ago and Danny mentioned it. He thought it was a very good offer, Jack."

"I'm a Chicago guy," Jack said. "I'll always be a Chicago guy. I'd hate L.A."

In truth, the job was something he might have seriously considered if it hadn't been for his ties to his family in Chicago. There was only so far he could go as a sports columnist. But this was a broadcast commentating gig along with the possibility of his own show on the nation's top-rated sports network. He'd have guests and he'd be able to interview players live and on camera.

Instead, he'd put it out of his mind completely, knowing he couldn't move away from his mother and sisters. There'd been other offers in the past and the answer had always been the same—no, not now.

But maybe the time was coming to make some changes. He'd been in a rut lately and now that he and Melanie had moved on, and his mother was newly independent, it was something he could consider.

He'd never really thought about life without
any worries or responsibilities, a life where he
was completely free to make his own choices.
Everything had always been about the family,
making sure everyone was healthy and happy
and secure.

"Maybe you ought to talk to them first before
you reject the possibilities," Elyse suggested.

"Maybe I should." Still, he'd feel a lot better if
his mother wasn't just scraping by on her teacher's pension. But a new job would pay more, so
he could hire someone to fix things around her
house when needed. And he'd only be a plane
ride away.

A knock sounded on the door and they both
turned to see Ben standing on the other side of
the screen. "Hello, there," he said, nodding at
Jack.

"Morning," Jack said.

"Mia went out to the bakery this morning.
We're having breakfast next to the pool if you'd
like to join us."

"I'll be out as soon as I dry my hair," Elyse
said, her smile wide and her eyes sparkling.

"I could eat," Jack said. He walked to the
door and stepped outside, then headed toward
the pool, Ben following behind. Though he'd
only been away from Mia for a short time, he
found himself wondering how she was doing.

As he approached the pool, her father called out. "Look who I found," Ben said. "Jack was up and about."

Mia gave him a coy smile. "Morning. Did you sleep well?"

"Like a baby," he said. Jack pulled out the chair beside her and sat down and Mia handed him the plate of pastries. He grabbed a cheese danish and bit into it. "Did you make these yourself?"

Mia laughed. "I was up all night baking."

"Is that what you call it?" he murmured.

"Well," Ben said. "I'm glad to see that you two are getting along so well. Elyse and I are driving up to Sonoma for the farmer's market and then we'd planned to check out a friend's winery. Would you two like to tag along? It will be fun, the four of us."

"No." They both answered at the same time, glancing at each other, then turning their attention back to Ben.

"Actually, I have some work to do," Jack said. "I have to watch the Cubs game and work on my next column."

"And I have work, as well," Mia said brightly. "But you two go along and have fun."

Ben got to his feet and held out his hand to Elyse as she approached. "I think we'll do just that. Are you ready my dear?"

Elyse smiled. "Absolutely. Let's go."

Jack and Mia watched as their parents walked back toward the house. "They were awfully anxious to get rid of us," she murmured.

"I know," he replied. "And they look a little too happy for my tastes. Did your father tell you that they were up until four this morning? My mother said they were talking. I don't know if I believe that."

"Do you think he's kissed her?" Mia asked.

"No," he said. "She would have mentioned it."

"Really?" Mia asked. "You and your mother talk about things like that? My father still thinks I'm a virgin."

Jack raised his eyebrow. "Are you?"

"No!"

"Because, if you were, I could help you do something about that. Just say the word."

Mia picked up a powdered sugar donut and threw it at him. The pastry hit him in the face, exploding in a shower of white powder. With a tiny scream, she leaped to her feet and ran away, but Jack was quicker. When he caught her, he grabbed her around the waist and pulled her body to his.

His lips found hers and he drew her into a long, deep kiss. She melted into his embrace and when they finally paused to take a breath, she looked up at him. "Your place or mine?"

"I don't know," he said. "What do you think?"

"I have a better idea." She grabbed his hand and pulled him along to a small pathway, cutting through lush foliage and a thick cover of trees. A small clearing opened up and Jack found himself staring at an ornate glass garden house. Mia ran ahead and opened the French doors until the entire house was filled with the morning breeze.

Then she led him inside. "My parents used to have parties out here when we were kids," she said. "They'd all lounge around drinking cocktails and dancing. My sisters and I would watch from the woods." Mia pulled him down on a wide, comfortable chaise, upholstered in a flowered fabric. "I had my first kiss out here when I was sixteen, at my birthday party."

"How did that go?" Jack asked, brushing his lips across hers in a teasing way as he braced himself above her.

"I'm sure you can do better."

He stretched out beside her, dragging her body against his. She wore a simple sleeveless dress and as he ran his hands over her body, he realized that all she wore beneath it was a pair of panties. Pulling her on top of him, he smoothed his hands around her waist. "There is one thing we forgot," he murmured.

She reached into the pocket of her dress and

pulled out a small plastic package. "I came prepared."

He laughed. "Good girl."

IT WAS THE PERFECT WAY to make love, Mia mused. They had the entire day in front of them so there was no need to rush. And Jack seemed to enjoy a lazy pace. They didn't bother to undress each other. Instead, they merely brushed clothing aside to touch and explore.

He was gentle and sweet and then suddenly, desperate and determined. It felt as if she were riding a roller-coaster, with passionate highs and languid lows, making her breathless with every moment that passed.

He explored her body with his hands and his lips, kissing her, trailing his damp tongue across her naked breast. Her body ached for the feel of his skin on hers.

Mia twisted her fingers in the faded T-shirt, then pulled it over his head. He was hard and ready, the ridge of his erection visible through the fabric of his shorts. Mia reached down to touch him, running her fingertips along his shaft.

He groaned softly and she smiled to herself. Mia hadn't had that much experience with men. She'd had lovers in the past, but the sex had never been very exciting. But with Jack, she already knew that past inhibitions had slipped away. Maybe she'd been too young or too insecure. But she was twenty-five years old now, a grown woman, and she knew exactly what she wanted.

A soft morning breeze blew through the gazebo sending a shiver skittering along her spine. But she wasn't cold or frightened of what was about to happen. Every nerve in her body was ready, anticipating the untold pleasure that she was about to experience.

Her dress had become a distraction. Frustrated, Mia pushed up onto her knees and reached for the hem, then slowly revealed her nearly naked body. Jack smiled as he took in the sight of her, appreciation evident in the gleam in his blue eyes. Tossing her hair over her shoulder, Mia bent close and kissed him.

They'd have this day and night together. Sometime tomorrow, she'd drive him to the airport and he'd leave. There was every chance that she'd never see him again. But what if that wasn't true? What if this was more than just a passing affair?

It would call into question her reasoning. She wanted something simple and uncomplicated, something that would shake her out of her doldrums and put her life as a woman back on track. She wanted to think of herself as sexy and exciting, the kind of woman who'd take risks with her love life and spend a little time on the edge.

But if she allowed herself to have more than just a sexual attraction for Jack Quinn, she was putting herself in danger. He was funny and sweet and exactly the kind of man a girl could fall in love with. But that wasn't what she wanted right now. She wanted passion without any strings attached. Mia wanted to be the kind of woman who could take what she needed from a man and then walk away.

He wanted to take his time, but suddenly Mia wanted to rush, to make sure she didn't back out. Were the tremors coursing through her body fear or excitement?

When she reached between them to stroke him through the fabric of his shorts, he groaned softly. But as with her dress, the clothing soon became a hindrance. Mia shimmied off him and then hooked her fingers around the waistband and pulled the shorts off.

When he was naked, lying beside her, Mia slowly took stock of the man she was about to seduce. He was beautiful, his body finely muscled, his limbs long and lean. She'd imagined a man like this in her bed—flawless, powerful and irresistible. But never in her wildest dreams had Mia believed the fantasy would come true.

Though the foreplay was enticing and exciting, Mia couldn't wait any longer. She found the condom she'd given him and tore open the package, then smoothed it over his shaft. He watched her silently, as if trying to understand her impatience. But when she pulled him on top of her, he didn't hesitate.

In one delicious surge, he settled himself between her legs and inside her body. The sensation took her breath away and Mia gasped. For a long time, he didn't move. Instead, he just kissed her gently, continuing to quietly seduce her with his lips.

Mia was so caught up in his kiss that she barely noticed when he began to move inside her. Each stroke was so slow and long. But then his rhythm increased and she found herself caught in an inexorable journey to her release. She couldn't ignore the need building inside her any more than she could stop herself from drawing breath.

Every movement seemed to twist at the knot deep in her core, creating a tantalizing pressure and search for satisfaction.

When he rolled her over and settled her on top of him, Mia knew she was lost. Now she was completely in control, able to follow every tempting path, to slow or quicken her release as she wanted. His hands rested on her hips, his fingers splayed over her flesh, but Jack let her set the pace.

It came upon her quickly, without any warning. Mia tried to stop herself, but the moment her body dissolved into deep and overwhelming spasms, she was lost. Jack followed her, his body arching into hers with each thrust until he tumbled over the edge.

When she was sated, Mia collapsed against his chest, her body shuddering with the after-effects of her orgasm. Jack smoothed the hair from her face and when she finally looked up at him, he smiled.

"That was fun," he said.

"I know," Mia replied.

"I could spend the whole day out here. Sleeping. Making love to you. Sleeping a little more."

"Don't you have a ball game to watch?" she asked.

"Not if I have better things to do," he said.

It didn't take a genius to see where this was going. One long marathon day of fabulous sex with Jack. They'd discover that they were perfect together, that they were the only people in the world that could satisfy each other's desires. She'd memorize every detail of every caress and every kiss and before she knew it, Mia would be falling in love with him—after just one day in bed.

She wasn't going to do that to herself. Mia pushed up on her elbow. She knew how vulnerable she was. Months of loneliness had made her desperate for any type of affection, even a wildy inappropriate one-night stand. But that was all this was supposed to be. One. Once and done.

"I was thinking we could go to the farmer's market," she said.

Jack frowned. "Really?"

"Yeah. There's a baker there that makes the best bread. I thought I could pick up some things and make a nice dinner tonight since this is going to be your last night here."

"I'd rather stay right here with you and send out for pizza."

"Come on," she teased. "We can't waste this beautiful day lying around. We'll have fun. I promise."

He studied her for a long moment and Mia was afraid he'd see the truth in her eyes. So she grabbed her dress and pulled it over her head. "I'm going to change and I'll meet you out front in fifteen minutes."

She dropped a quick kiss on his lips and then ran out of the gazebo and down the path toward the pool. By the time she reached the house, she was breathless. Mia leaned back against the door and closed her eyes. She'd thought sex with Jack would be the answer to all her problems.

In reality, it just created more.

"You have to taste one of these," Mia said. "They are so wonderful, you'll cry."

It was the opening day for the farmer's market, located in the quaint town of Napa in the middle of California's wine country. The drive out through the countryside had been lovely, the sky clear, the temperature rising as noon approached. Jack had sat back and enjoyed the ride while Mia drove, giving him tourist commentary on everything they passed.

Though she might be able to put aside what had happened in the gazebo, Jack couldn't stop thinking about it. Images of her naked body kept intruding on his thoughts and though he tried to concentrate on the moment at hand, he couldn't keep from wondering whether they'd be together again.

When they'd arrived in the pretty village of Napa, Mia had parked the car and they'd set off in search of breakfast—or lunch. The atmosphere had been festive, as if the reappearance of the market was the official start of summer, even though it was only the first week in May.

Mia looked like summer, wearing a breezy cotton dress that fell to her slender calves. She'd twisted a scarf through her flaxen hair and her pretty toes peeked out from a pair of sandals. But all Jack could think about was whether she was wearing underwear.

He'd had more than one moment of regret that they hadn't stayed in the gazebo and taken advantage of an entire day alone. But the more he got to know Mia, the more he cared about her. And was it really fair to take advantage of their sexual attraction, knowing that he was going back to Chicago in just twenty-four hours?

She held the pastry out in front of him. "What is it?" he asked.

"Just taste first," she said.

He looked at the small roll and bit into it, then smiled. The flaky pastry was filled with sausage. "Oh, now that's good. We need to buy more of those. I could eat them all day."

"English sausage rolls," she said. "But we have to pace ourselves. If you like to eat, this place can be dangerous."

They bought three more rolls, then continued their walk through the stalls and tents, stopping at each vendor to look at the products offered. Even though they expected to run into Ben and Elyse, they hadn't really made any attempt to find them. Actually, Jack was glad to have time alone to learn a little bit more about the woman who'd occupied his fantasies for almost an entire day.

"Chicago is a town made for foodies," he said.

"I know. I've been there. I could spend a week eating through the pizza."

"Do you get to Chicago very often?" Jack asked.

"Once or twice a year," she said with a shrug. "I have a client who owns a couple of restaurants, one here and one in Chicago. I do all the graphic design for them."

"What's the name of the restaurant?"

"Caravello's," she said.

"That's about seven or eight blocks from my place," he said. "The next time you come, I'll have to take you out and show you the town."

For some reason, the thought of seeing her on his turf made him feel as if there might be something more between them, something to look forward to. Even now, he could picture her, walking along the streets of his neighborhood, stopping by his favorite coffee shop, chatting with him as they read the morning papers, sitting beside him in the press box at a Cubs or Blackhawks game.

"I'll be sure to call you the next time I'm in Chicago," she said.

"Give me your cell phone," he said, holding out his hand. She handed it to him and he quickly put his number into her lists of contacts. "There.

Now you'll have no excuses. You have my number."

She stared down at the number on the phone, then smiled. "All right. But you need to have my number." She hit a few buttons on her phone and a moment later, his rang.

Chuckling, Jack pulled it out of his pocket. "Hello."

"Hello," she said, smiling coyly. "It's me. Next we'll be moving on to a place that makes the most delicious wild mushroom tarts. The crust is so buttery, you won't be able to stop at one bite."

He grabbed her hand and laced his fingers through hers, slipping his phone back into his pocket. Jack stared down at their hands, unable to tell whose fingers were whose. Holding hands was such a simple thing, but yet it represented a giant admission to them both. They enjoyed the physical contact. They needed it, even in a public place like this.

But a few seconds later, she pulled away and walked toward a booth that sold kitchen supplies. Jack trailed after her, determined to continue the conversation.

"You know, I get out to California fairly regularly, as well. In fact, I'll be back in San Francisco next month when the Cubs play the Giants. I think you need to come to a ball game with me."

"Maybe," she said. Jack watched as she picked

up a ladle and examined it. He got the distinct sense that something was bothering her, but he was almost afraid to ask what it was. Was she worried about her father and his mother? Or were her concerns about the two of them? Maybe she was just tired.

He stood next to her and picked up a spatula. "This is nice."

"It is," she murmured.

"So, what's the problem here, Mia. Are you really not interested in seeing me again after I leave? Was I just good for a roll in the hay and that's it?"

She dropped the ladle onto the table with a clatter then spun around to face him. "What? No!" Mia shook her head. "Why would you think that?"

"Listen, I understand if that's the way it is. I can handle the whole no-strings, friends-with-benefits approach. Okay, so I might feel a little used, but I can accept that."

"I would never—"

Jack bent close and stopped her words with a long, lingering kiss. "But," he murmured, "just in case you aren't aware, I enjoy your company, Mia. And I wouldn't be opposed to spending a little more time together—if we could."

"You wouldn't?" she asked, her eyes wide and searching.

"I wouldn't. What about you?"

"All right."

"All right?" he repeated.

A pretty blush rose on her cheeks. "I would, too."

Jack chuckled. "And here, I thought you were just using me for sex."

"I was," Mia said. "But this is good, too. I think." She spied a tent and her face lit up. "There. These are the tarts."

Mia pulled him along until they reached the table and she ordered a mushroom tart and an onion tart. They were wrapped in paper and she held one out for him to take a bite. The egg was like custard, rich and creamy, and the mushrooms were earthy and flavorful.

Jack groaned softly. Every moment with Mia seemed like a delight for the senses. Between the sex, the food and the breathtaking scenery around them, he was constantly off-kilter. "You are a very dangerous woman," he said after he swallowed. "More."

She offered him another bite and he nodded. "So good."

"Me or the tart?"

"Aren't you the tart? Oh, wait. No. You're talking about the quiche?"

She slapped him playfully. "The onion is good, too."

He leaned forward to take a bite, but at the last moment, shifted and kissed her lips. They were buttery from the pastry and she tasted delicious. A giggle slipped from her lips and he drew back. "One more taste, my little tart," he murmured. But her body stiffened suddenly and he drew back. "Was the joke that bad?"

"My dad and your mom," she whispered.

Jack quickly dropped his hands to his sides and watched as Ben and Elyse approached. It wasn't clear from their expressions whether they'd seen what had just happened or not.

"You decided to come, after all," Elyse said. "We're so glad."

"The farmer's market sounded like such a good idea," Mia explained. "And you know how much I love these tarts. I can't get enough of them."

"Sausage rolls," Jack murmured. "She likes the sausage rolls, too."

"I just thought I'd pick up some things and make us all dinner tonight," Mia continued, "since it's your last night here."

Ben glanced at Elyse, then slipped his arm around her waist. "Not exactly true, sweetheart. I've asked Elyse to stay for the rest of the week. There's still so much that we want to see and do together. A weekend is barely enough time to get reacquainted. We can do dinner tomorrow night. Tonight, we're going out for a night on the town."

Elyse's eyes were bright with excitement.

"What about Jack?" Mia blurted out. She glanced over at him, as if she'd surprised even herself. Clearing her throat, she forced a smile. "Of course, you're welcome to stay, too," she said to him. "Isn't he, Daddy?"

Elyse shook her head. "Oh, I'm sure Jack has to get back to Chicago for work. But thank you for the invitation, Mia."

Ben looked at him. "Of course, you're welcome to stay if you'd like, Jack. I can't say there'll be much for you to do unless you want to tag along with us. But the guest cottage is yours for the week if you'd like to relax a little longer."

"Really, I'm sure he has work," Elyse insisted, sending Jack a warning look. It was obvious she didn't want him to stay. But this invitation from Ben was troublesome. Something was changing between Mia's father and his mother and Jack wasn't sure he liked the look of it.

Jack shrugged. "No, I can take some time. I think I would like to stay a little longer. I have some business in L.A. that I can take care of while I'm here." He turned to Mia. "And I don't want to miss this dinner you're going to cook for all of us."

"Great," Ben said. "So, I guess we'll leave

the two of you to your shopping and we'll get on with our winery tour." He grabbed Elyse's hand and drew her along with him. "You two have a pleasant day. Enjoy yourselves."

They vanished almost as fast as they appeared, leaving Jack and Mia standing in the middle of a crowd. "Do you get the sense that they really didn't want us tagging along with them?" Jack asked.

"Yeah," Mia said. "I think they wanted to be alone."

"What do you think that means?"

Mia glanced over at him. "I don't know. But I can't imagine it will be good for either one of us."

## 4

MIA SAT ON THE EDGE OF the pool and watched as Jack swam from one end to the other. When he popped up in front of her, he grabbed her bare foot and gave it a kiss.

"Don't tease me," she said.

"You like it."

They'd left the farmer's market and drove directly back to the house, Mia no longer interested in shopping for the dinner she'd planned. Her father's invitation to Elyse had changed everything. She could certainly rationalize a weekend get-together between two friends, but this was different. It was clear her father had more than friendship in mind.

And what about Jack? Exactly what were his intentions? Though she'd been the one to actually offer the invitation to him, she'd never thought he'd accept. She'd hoped. And when he had, Mia was forced to wonder why. Was he staying to keep an eye on his mother? Or was he staying to spend more time with her?

"Are we going to talk about this?" Mia asked.

"What?" he asked. "My growing obsession with your beautiful feet? Or my need to undress you and drag you into this pool with me?" He held out his hand. "Come on, Mia, the water is perfect."

"I'm talking about our parents," she said.

"What about them?"

"You aren't worried that they're getting a little serious with each other?"

"Are you?" Jack asked.

"Yes," she said. "I don't want my father to make a mistake. I think he's very vulnerable and he might misread your mother's affections for more than they actually are. He's a very wealthy man and there are plenty of women who'd take advantage of that."

Jack stared at her for a long moment, then shook his head. "You think my mother is a gold digger? Is that what you're saying?"

"No." She cursed softly. "But you can't deny that marrying my father would make her life a lot easier. She'd never have to worry about money again."

"Well, you don't have to worry," Jack said. "Your father's money is safe. My mother would never agree to marry him, anyway. She'll never leave Chicago. And your father won't leave California. It's a no-win situation."

"You don't seem concerned at all," Mia said.

"Maybe I wouldn't mind if my mother found someone to love," he said. "I just don't want to see her hurt and if your dad is just playing around her, I'm not going to be happy."

"My father would never do that. He's a stand-up guy."

"I'm not saying he isn't. But you seem to think my mother is only interested in your dad's money. Can't I have some legitimate concerns about your father's motives?"

"No!" Mia cried. She got to her feet and paced along the edge of the pool. "You have no idea what he's been through. Years of dealing with my mother's illness.... He was always there, by her side, determined to make her well with just the power of his love for her." Mia turned and walked toward the house, then stopped to say one last thing. "Your mother would be lucky if he fell in love with her!"

"Oh, yeah?" Jack shouted. "Well, I could say the same for your father!"

Mia strode back to the house, her temper barely in check. She'd always known there might come a day when her father would move on. And she, along with her sisters, had hoped that the day wouldn't come at all. It wasn't that she didn't want her father to be happy, she just didn't want to believe that he could put his life with her mother in the past.

She couldn't imagine how painful it would be to watch him lavish the same affections on another woman—a woman who wasn't her mother. Holidays, family birthdays, family vacations would all be irrevocably different with someone else at his side.

She was being selfish, Mia knew. But she had a right, didn't she? She was protecting the memory of her mother. Mia opened the screen door and walked into the kitchen, then stopped short.

But what was Jack doing? Did he really approve of a possible relationship between their parents? She'd just assumed they were on the same side. But there was no question that he was more open than she was to the notion that his mother and her father might fall in love.

She grabbed a couple of bottles of water from the fridge and then decided it would be best to confront him about his opinions. After all, if they were going to be on opposite sides of this issue, it would be best to know it up front.

When she got back to the pool, Jack was stretched out on a chaise, his sunglasses hiding his eyes. She wasn't sure if he'd spotted her, but when she stood next to his chair, he turned his head. "Feeling better?" he asked.

Mia shrugged. "I wasn't feeling bad. Just a little...perturbed."

"Nice word," he said.

"I brought you some water." She held out the bottle. "And I'm sorry if I got snippy with you. The subject of my father finding a new wife brings out the worst in me."

He reached out, but instead of grabbing the bottle, he wrapped his fingers around her wrist and gently pulled her down on top of him.

"Do you think it's strange that I worry so much about him?" Mia asked, snuggling against Jack's body.

"No, I'm the last one to say that." He paused. "My mother told me that it's time I started thinking more about myself and less about taking care of the family. I'm starting to think that she's right."

"You lost your father when you were so young," Mia said. "I can see how that might have changed the way you look at things."

"I just never thought of putting myself first. It was never about what I wanted. It was always about what was best for my mom and younger sisters." He shook his head. "But they've been all right for a long time. And I've been using them as an excuse."

"An excuse for what?"

"For not making any real commitments in my life. For not taking any risks." Jack pulled her closer. "I need to let go of that responsibility," he said. "Whatever happens with my mother, it's her life. I have my own life to live."

Jack pulled her closer and kissed her gently, his tongue tracing along the line between her lips. She opened for him and the kiss deepened, his mouth possessing hers with such desire that Mia felt her doubts melt away.

When he finally drew back, Mia sighed softly. "I understand how you feel," she murmured. "But I'm just not there yet. It's too soon. And it has nothing to do with your mother. She's lovely. It has to do with me and my own…insecurities."

"I understand," he said. "We can agree to disagree."

"You're not angry?"

Jack shook his head. "No. Now, can we stop talking about our parents' love lives and start talking about ours?"

"We don't have a love life," Mia said.

"I'm thinking we might want to work on that. Since I'm staying until the end of the week, we're going to have to find something to occupy our time."

Mia pushed up on her elbow and stared down at him. She reached out and slid the sunglasses up so she could see his eyes. The teasing glint was obvious and a smile curled the corners of her mouth. "Do you really think that would be a good idea?"

"I think it would be an excellent idea," Jack said. "I'd like to discuss this 'friends with benefits' suggestion of yours."

"I may have been mistaken about that," Mia said.

"Maybe you weren't."

She drew a deep breath. "There have to be some rules," she said. "First, and most important, we can't fall in love."

"And why is that?" Jack asked.

"Because, I'm just not ready to deal with the inevitable breakup. I'm not sure I'm strong enough to survive that right now."

"Not everyone breaks up," he said.

"Yes, they do," Mia countered. "Unless you fall in love forever, you break up. And I know I'm not ready to fall in love forever, so that only leaves breaking up." She stared down into his eyes. "We can only do this if you promise you won't have any expectations. At the end of the week, we'll just say goodbye and get on with our lives."

"And if I'm in town and I want to take you to a ball game?" Jack asked.

"We'll figure that one out when it happens,"

she said. Then she drew a deep breath and let it out in a sigh. "My life really is a mess," she murmured.

"Mine, too," Jack said. "I thought I'd have everything sorted out by the time I was thirty."

"When do you turn thirty?"

"I did. Last August."

She paused. "My family is giving me a pass for now. I've been the caretaker for the past six years so I haven't really had the time," she said.

"So that explains it," he said.

"Explains what?"

"Why someone as beautiful as you isn't already married. Or at least in a relationship."

"Dating can be exhausting. That's why our arrangement is so much better. All the good stuff without the bad."

Jack laughed out loud, then reached out and grabbed her hand, lacing his fingers through hers. He pressed a kiss to the back of her hand. "It is good, isn't it," he murmured.

A shiver skittered down her spine and Mia curled up against his body. Yes, it was good. Better than she'd ever expected. It was going to be difficult for her to keep from falling head over heels. But she'd just have to keep the realities of the situation in mind. Jack lived in Chicago and she lived here. Anything more than just no-strings sex would be impossible.

SHE WAS ALL SWEET SCENT and soft flesh. After playing in the pool for a couple of hours, they decided to get out of the sun, finding shade in the empty guest cottage. Jack couldn't seem to get enough of her and as they rolled around on his bed, he felt like a horny teenager in the throes of his first sexual experience.

He usually prided himself on his self-control, his ability to seduce slowly and thoroughly. But with Mia, it seemed as if they were racing against the clock, trying to satisfy needs and desires that would suddenly expire in twenty-four hours.

But he wasn't leaving. He'd be staying with her for the rest of the week. There would be time to explore every corner of their desire, to test the limits of their passion. But even that thought didn't make him more patient.

She was dressed in a simple bikini, modest by most standards. But from the moment they'd tumbled onto the bed in a tangle of sun-warmed limbs and damp hair, he'd wanted to rid them both of anything resembling clothing. An image of her naked body had been floating in his memory since their morning in the gazebo and he felt almost desperate to prove to himself that she was as beautiful as he remembered.

Mia watched him as he untied the knot at the front of her top, her gaze fixed on his face, her fingers running through his hair. When the fabric fell away, he bent close and pressed his mouth to the soft flesh of her breast. Then Jack slipped his arm around her waist and pulled her body up off the bed, pressing his mouth to the curve of her neck as she arched beneath him.

"Was it really just this morning that we did this?" he murmured, glancing up at her.

Mia nodded. "It seems like days ago, doesn't it? I can't stop thinking about you…about this."

"What if it never goes away?" Jack asked.

"I don't know," she said. "I guess it will be a memory then."

Jack smiled. He knew how she felt. From the moment he'd first touched her, they'd been racing toward the inevitable. He kissed his way back up to her lips, then pulled her down beside him.

He hooked his finger around the hip of her bikini bottom and pulled it down, past her knees and over her ankles. And after he tossed it aside, he slipped out of his board shorts.

Their bodies fit together perfectly as Jack pulled her beneath him, catching her mouth in a long, deep kiss. He wanted to make sure they savored every moment, every soft caress, every delicious kiss, every inch of naked flesh.

"Jack? Are you in here?"

His mother's voice echoed through the guest

cottage and they both sat up and stared at the bedroom door. They'd left it open and unlocked. Mia jumped up from the bed, dragging the sheet around her body. Jack cursed softly, scrambling to find his board shorts.

"Closet," Mia said. She ran over and pulled open the door, then stepped inside. But instead of waiting to talk to his mother, Jack stepped inside the closet with Mia and closed the door behind him.

"What are you doing in here? You should be out there," Mia said.

The walk-in closet was dark, but Jack found her almost immediately. "Shhhh," he whispered. "She won't find us in here."

"There's no lock on—"

He covered her mouth with his, stopping her warning with a delicious kiss, his tongue teasing at hers until she reluctantly gave in and kissed him back. He pressed her back against the wall, his hands running over her body as if his touch could imprint her image in his head.

Mia moaned softly as he got to the damp spot between her legs. Even in the dark, he found all of his favorite spots—the indentation at the small of her back, the sweet curve of her hip, the soft flesh of her backside.

His stiff shaft rubbed against her belly and every time she moved, he felt the desire snake through him like a current of electricity. Like their night in the car, they were completely isolated, the world around them limited to the space within their touch.

Jack kissed a trail from her collarbone to her breast and then moved lower still. Mia clutched at his hair, her fingers twisting in the strands, slowing his progress when he found a particularly enjoyable spot. But Jack knew exactly how he wanted to pleasure her.

He found the place again, the core of her desire, damp and warm between her thighs. His tongue delved between the soft folds, flicking at the tiny nub. Jack heard her breath catch, as if he'd surprised her by what he'd done.

"We can't," she whispered.

"The condoms are on the other side of the door," he murmured, slipping a finger inside her. Her knees buckled slightly and Mia braced her hands on his shoulders as she arched against him.

Jack seduced her slowly, knowing that they couldn't leave the safety of the closet until they were alone again in the cottage. She whispered his name, softly, urgently, and then she dissolved into her release. Her body trembled as each spasm washed through her and she struggled to stay upright.

When she was finally finished, her knees collapsed and she sank down onto the floor. A tiny giggle slipped from her lips. "You are so bad," she whispered. "In a really good way."

He drew her into his arms. "This is the first time I've done it in a closet."

"I'm so happy to know I could help you with that." She pushed him down onto the floor and crawled on top of him. "What are we going to do while we wait?"

"My bag is in here. I might have some snacks."

"Chocolate?"

"Maybe. Let me see what I can find." He rolled out from under her, searching the floor of the closet. He found his computer bag first and dug through it, then pulled out a penlight and flipped it on. "Now that's better," he said, shining it in her face.

He held the light in his teeth and dumped the bag out on the floor. "Gameboy," he said, holding it out to her. "I think it's hockey. My baseball stats book. My press pass. And…bubble gum. I have bubble gum. The catcher from the Cubs gave this to me. It's his own special brand."

"I'll take the gum," she said, holding out her hand. "How long do you think we can survive on the gum?"

"I don't know. But I'm pretty sure we can make it. Aren't they supposed to go out for dinner and *Doctor Zhivago* tonight?"

"I think so. What if they decided not to go? What if they're too tired?"

"Then we'll have to spend the night in here. It will be tough, but I think I can handle it."

Mia crawled over to him and wrapped them both in the sheet she'd pulled from the bed. "If I have to be trapped in a closet with a naked man, I'm really happy it's you."

They curled up together, leaning up against the wall, her naked body tucked against his. Jack had never really experienced a relationship quite as odd as this one. Nothing ever seemed to go precisely as planned. But then, there was a certain excitement to that. With Mia, he never knew what to expect.

Actually, that was one of the things Jack liked most about Mia. She kept life interesting.

They stayed in the closet for another fifteen minutes, then quietly opened the door and listened for any sound coming from the direction of his mother's room. But the guest cottage was silent.

Jack reached down and grabbed her hand, then pulled her to her feet. After checking to make sure they were alone, they ran out into the bedroom and jumped onto his bed, rolling around until they were twisted in the bedclothes. "I'm thinking that maybe I should think about other living arrangements while I'm here."

"Where are you going to go?"

"I have to go down to L.A. for a day or two. Maybe you could come with me. We could make a little vacation of it? Or what about staying at your place in the city?"

"Do you really think we should leave our parents alone?" Mia asked.

"I'm pretty sure we're not going to find them naked in a closet," he said.

"Ew," Mia cried, covering her ears with her hands. "Don't even say that! You can't say things like that!" She paused. "I just hope he doesn't get hurt."

"I know," Jack said.

"That's why the friends-with-benefits plan is so good. No matter what happens, our emotions aren't involved."

Even now, after just a few days with Mia, Jack knew that he wasn't going to be able to walk away without a few regrets. And the more time he spent with her, the more attached he became. He'd take his chances, but with Mia, it was certain to be all or nothing. But who said it had to be nothing?

MIA LEANED OVER THE counter and stared at the coffeemaker, waiting for it to fill enough to steal a mug. She fought back a yawn, but couldn't help herself. After their official good-night at eleven, when their parents finally got home, Mia and Jack had decided to wait a few hours and meet up in the gazebo. They'd spent the next three hours lost in passionate pursuits before Jack snuck back to the guest cottage to pretend that he'd been asleep there all along.

Though she and Jack were perfectly capable of making their own decisions about their sex life, she couldn't help but feel a little guilty sneaking around as if they were doing something wrong. Jack was right. They needed to come up with a new plan.

"Good morning, Mimi. It looks like you slept late."

She turned around to find her dad standing behind her, fresh from a shower and looking well-rested. "Morning, Daddy. You're walking without the crutches."

"My ankle is feeling much better today. I might even be up for a game of tennis. I thought I might teach Elyse to play."

She straightened, shaking her head. "Daddy, you need to be careful. The doctor said you strained your ligaments."

"I'm perfectly fine, Mimi," he said, using the nickname he always called her when they were alone. "And I will be careful." He wandered over to the fridge and grabbed a small carton of cream, then stood next to her and joined her in watching the coffee. "I'm glad I caught you before you left for the day. I wanted to talk to you."

Mia held her breath. What was this about? Had he somehow found out about her and Jack? Or was he going to tell her something about himself and Elyse? She grabbed the coffeepot and carried it over to the table, pouring them both a cup before they sat down.

"I'm sorry about leaving you to entertain Elyse's son," Ben said.

Entertain? Is that what he thought she was doing with Jack? She couldn't help but smile. "It's no problem, Daddy. He's a nice guy."

"That's what I wanted to talk to you about," he said.

"What's wrong?" Mia asked, sitting up straight.

"Elyse has talked quite a bit about Jack and his relationship with Melanie."

"Melanie?"

"His long-term girlfriend. It's all over now, but according to Elyse, it was serious." He shook his head. "I just get the sense that Jack is the kind of guy who just can't commit. It seems like there's an attraction between you two and I just think you need to know that there's really no future with a man like him. He's looking for something he'll never find."

"And you think I want a future?"

"Of course you do. Look at how happy your sisters are. They want the same for you—marriage and children, a home with a man you love."

"Maybe I don't want that. At least not now."

"Sweetheart, I know you. You've always been far too trusting when it comes to men. I'm just asking you to maintain a safe distance with this one. Don't let yourself get caught up in his charms."

"All right," Mia said. In truth, after last night, she'd decided that sex with Jack Quinn was far more dangerous than she ever thought it would be. She spent the early morning hours tossing and turning, fighting the urge to sneak out of the house and crawl through his bedroom window in the guest cottage to enjoy more of what he had to offer.

She'd built a whole scenario in her head. She'd stand beside his bed and take off her clothes and, sometime during the silent striptease, he'd wake up. He'd sit up in bed and watch her and then, once she was finished, he'd hold back the covers and she'd crawl in beside his naked body.

After that, the fantasy became all too real in her head, a long, delicious exploration that led to multiple orgasms for both of them.

"Good morning!"

Her father stood and watched as Elyse walked in the back door. Mia ignored a sliver of irritation at the woman's ease at entering her father's house. She hadn't even knocked. Wasn't that customary?

Elyse crossed the kitchen and when she reached Ben's side, she pushed up on her toes and gave him a kiss on the cheek. "Good morning," she said, saving an intimate smile for him.

Mia's gaze darted back and forth between the two of them, examining their expressions. She felt her spirits sink at the affection they were both showing.

"You look lovely this morning." Ben leaned close and kissed her cheek. "Are you ready to go?"

"Go?" Mia asked. "Where are you two going now? Don't you just want to sit still every now and then?"

"We have all sorts of plans for today," Ben said. "I'm taking Elyse to the plant so I can show her around our offices. Then we're going to drive to Santa Cruz for the afternoon. Tonight, we're going dancing on the roof of the Bellingham. And we'd really like it if you and Jack could meet us there."

"Oh, Daddy, I'm not really a dancing kind of girl. And I don't think Jack is—"

"Mimi, you don't have to dance. You can listen to the music, have a few drinks. It's important that you come."

"But—"

"Jack was still asleep when I left," Elyse said with a sweet smile. "Let him know where we went, will you? Your father says you play tennis. You two should play. Jack's a pretty decent player."

"My Mimi played in college," Ben said. "We'll see you later." Ben took Elyse's hand and they headed off toward the front door.

"Sure," Mia called. "Have fun." As soon as they were out of sight, she hurried to the guest cottage. She slipped inside and went to the smaller bedroom then knocked softly on the door. When there wasn't an answer, she opened the door.

"Jack," she whispered. Mia shook her head. Why was she whispering. "Jack!"

"Yeah!"

She opened the door to find him sitting up in bed. Their activities from the previous evening flashed in her mind and she pressed her hand to her chest in an attempt to restart her heart. "Get up," she said.

"What time is it?"

"Eight-thirty."

He flopped back down on the bed. "What is that, six-thirty Chicago time?"

"No, it's ten-thirty Chicago time."

He frowned, raking his hand through his hair. "Why did I sleep so late?" A grin came across his expression. "Oh, yeah, I remember now. It's all your fault." Mia reached out and grabbed his hand to pull him out of bed, but instead, he tugged her down beside him. "Good morning, beautiful. Did you sleep well?"

"No, as a matter of fact, I didn't."

He smoothed his hands around her waist and pulled her close, but Mia wiggled away, sitting up on the edge of the bed. "We need to talk."

Jack frowned. "I hate when women say that. It's never anything good, like 'We have to talk— I won the lottery,' or 'We have to talk—of course you can buy that sports car.'"

"Our parents would like us to join them tonight in the city. They hold summer dances on the roof of the Bellingham Hotel and that's where they're going tonight."

"I don't dance," Jack said.

"Neither do I," Mia added. "And I told them that. But my father insisted that we be there." She paused. "He's taking her to see his company today. They're going to tour the plant and the office."

"That sounds…incredibly boring," Jack said. "Doesn't your dad's company make microchips?"

"Nano technology," she said.

"I'm sure we can find something much better to do with our time, don't you think? Maybe

I could take you to where I work. There's a Giants game today. We could go to the ballpark."

She scrambled to her feet and began to pace beside the bed. "Something is going on and I don't feel good about it," Mia said. "Why is he taking her to see the business? What is he trying to prove to her?"

Jack swung his legs off the bed and the covers fell away to reveal his dark blue boxer briefs. He yawned, stretching his arms over his head and Mia found her attention caught by the play of muscle across his chest and shoulders.

She loved the way his body looked and moved and felt beneath her hands. Mia shook her head, bringing her thoughts back to the matter at hand. "Is your mother always this active? My father has barely bothered to leave the house for anything but work since my mother died and now, he's running all over the countryside."

"She likes to do things," Jack said. "But she usually goes with friends. I wish she could travel more on a teacher's pension, that's not really an option. My sisters and I always buy her one big trip for Christmas every year. Last year it was China. The year before that, she went to Greece."

"My father used to love to travel," Mia murmured, slowing her pace. "And he and my mom were always going places and doing things."

Jack stared at her for a long moment. "They're

just having a good time, Mia. Just like we are—
only in their own way."

"I don't know," Mia replied. "I think there's
something there. I can feel it. He's happy again.
And I was beginning to wonder if that would
ever happen. Don't you see it?"

"Sure," Jack said. "I guess I do. But that
doesn't mean they're going to run off to Vegas
and get married tomorrow. You don't know my
mother. She takes a long time to make decisions.
It took her over a year to decide on a color to
paint her house and another year to decide if she
made the right decision. Marriage is nothing like
house paint. You can't change it all a year later
because you made the wrong decision—which
she did, by the way."

Mia shook her head. "Maybe I'm wrong.
Maybe I'm just imagining all of this." She
shrugged, then drew a deep breath. "It's all right.
I sometimes overreact. And I didn't get much
sleep last night, so that's not helping."

Jack closed his eyes and flopped back on the
bed. "You should know that I'm much lazier than
my mother. I'm thinking we should spend the
rest of the day in bed. What are your thoughts
on that?"

Mia stretched out beside him, nestling into
the curve of his arm and resting her hand on his
naked chest. "I don't know. Maybe we should get

out and do something. Just for the day. To put things in perspective. An afternoon of baseball might make an evening of rumbas and cha-chas much more tolerable."

Jack pushed up on his elbow and stared down into her eyes. "I think that's a perfect idea. Do you like baseball?"

"Sure. My dad always took us when we were younger. I know my way around a ballpark."

Jack crawled out of bed and walked to the bathroom. Mia followed him, then perched on the edge of the counter to watch him brush his teeth. As she took in every detail of his morning routine, she realized how intimate it all seemed. This was how it would be if they lived together, these simple tasks.

Some days, they'd get up early and rush to work. Other days, they'd get up late and shower together, brush their teeth, maybe have a cup of coffee still wrapped in towels.

And then, on Sundays, they'd fall back into bed for another session of mind-blowing sex. Mia wondered what it would take to make that happen right now. Perhaps if she just reached out and touched him. Her fingers twitched as she imagined her hands smoothing over wide shoulders, down his flat belly and then lower.

He rinsed his mouth and then tossed the tooth-brush on the counter. "Much better," he said.

Jack cupped her face in his hands and gave her a sweet and lingering kiss. And when it was over, he pressed his forehead to hers. "Good morning," he murmured.

"Morning," she said. Mia wrapped her arms around his neck. He tasted all minty and sweet and irresistible.

It was the perfect way to start the day, Mia mused. He grabbed her waist and then stepped between her legs. A shiver skittered over her body as he slipped his fingers through her hair.

His hands seemed to be everywhere at once and yet she felt as if every caress was drawn out to its absolute end. First her face and then her shoulders. When he tugged off her T-shirt and tossed it aside, his mouth found the base of her throat.

She didn't realize how much she craved these feelings, the excitement that raced through her body, the need and the longing. The only thing she wanted to think about was how they were going to get from the bathroom to his bed as quickly as possible.

The fabric of his boxer briefs outlined his growing erection and Mia knew her next move would tempt him even further. She reached out and skimmed her fingers over the front of his shorts.

His reaction was immediate and he groaned

softly, pressing his mouth against her throat. Then, he drew back and looked down into her eyes. "I can't seem to get enough of you," he whispered.

Mia smiled. "I know exactly how you feel."

Everything about him was perfect for her. He was sweet and strong and funny and kind. And from the moment she'd met him, she knew he was the kind of guy she could trust. It didn't matter what warnings her father gave her or what challenges she saw in the future. They were together now and she wanted to experience him completely, without any reservations.

"Maybe we could try it in the closet again," she teased. "Only, this time, with the lights on."

# 5

"YOU LOOK GOOD IN A HAT."

Jack reached over and adjusted the brim of the baseball cap, as the evening breeze buffeted the inside of the Mini Cooper, causing strands of her pale hair to blow around her pretty face.

They'd spent the afternoon at the ballpark, watching the Giants deal a loss to the Mets. The game was a badly needed distraction for Mia and Jack was glad of it. They cheered, they drank beer, they argued over calls and for Jack, it was a perfect afternoon. There hadn't been any talk about their parents.

In truth, it was the closest thing they'd had to a regular date. And the easy friendship that they shared was yet another piece in what was becoming a real relationship.

Jack knew he shouldn't project his own feelings onto an arrangement that Mia was controlling. She made the rules, she decided what they were now and what they might become in the future. But he could already see that it could work between them. They were wild about each other in the bedroom and he was just as wild about her outside of it.

"I had a good time today," Mia said. She glanced over at him and smiled. "Thanks for talking me into going."

"I told you, a ball game will always fix whatever ails you."

"You were right. I feel much better now."

Jack reached over and grabbed her hand, then kissed her fingertips, one by one. "I'm glad. I like to see you happy. You have a very pretty smile."

"You don't have to flatter me," she murmured.

"I'm not flattering you," he said. "I'm stating a fact."

Mia sighed softly. "Saying things like that only makes things harder."

"Maybe they should be hard," he said. "Maybe there's a reason for that."

"We decided that this was just going to be a temporary thing, remember? You can't change the rules halfway through the game. You should know that."

"Are we playing a game, Mia? Because, to me, it sure doesn't feel like one. It feels real."

As they sped along the Embarcadero, a wide thoroughfare lined with palm trees, silence descended between them. Jack stared out at the waterfront. He knew he shouldn't have pushed things. It was way too early. But their relationship had been one big runaway train from the very start and if he didn't slow it down now, Jack was afraid they'd crash and burn.

He'd found something with Mia that he hadn't had in the past, a deeper connection that he wanted to explore a little further. But how could he convince her to give them a chance?

Mia turned the car away from the water and headed up a long, steep hill. Though Jack had visited San Francisco many times while covering the Cubs, he hadn't spent a lot of time getting to know the city. Mia was perfectly comfortable here, he mused. This was her home in the same way Chicago was his.

She steered into the tiniest of parking spots on the street, then turned off the ignition. "This is it," she said. She hopped out of the car, then grabbed her bag from the backseat. Jack stepped out and looked up at the row house, wedged between two others of the exact same size and design. He climbed the front steps and waited as she unlocked the door to the stairs.

"I'm on the third floor."

They climbed the flights and when they got to

the top, Mia opened the door and stepped inside. Jack followed her, taking in the details of the interior. It was a bright and sunny apartment with a huge bay window that overlooked the street. The interior was beautifully decorated, so unlike the ordinary interior of his flat.

"It's nice," he murmured as he walked over to the window. He could imagine her here, living her life, coming home from work and relaxing with a glass of wine, making dinner for herself.

"Thanks," she said. "We're supposed to meet my dad and your mom at eight, so we have about an hour. I could make us something to eat."

"I wouldn't mind a shower," he said.

She stared at him for a long moment, then nodded her head. "Sure. It's this way."

"Wait," he said, slipping his hands around her waist. "Just wait for a second." Jack turned her to face him and Mia looked up into his gaze, her expression wary. When he bent closer, he felt her soften in his arms and Jack kissed her. Though his feelings for her grew more confused with every moment they spent together, he needed to know there was still an attraction between them.

"Maybe we should take a shower together," he suggested.

Mia smiled coyly. "Do you really want to start

something when we're supposed to be somewhere in an hour?"

"I can be very efficient," he murmured.

"I think we can test that another time," she
said. "The bathroom is down the hall on the left.
There are fresh towels in the closet next to the
sink. It takes about two minutes for the hot water
to make it from the ground floor to my flat, so
be patient."

Jack grabbed his bag and walked down
the hall. He'd brought along a clean shirt and
freshly-pressed khakis, more appropriate ward-
robe for a dance than cargo shorts and a T-shirt.
He closed the bathroom door behind him and
stripped out of his clothes, then turned on the
shower and waited for the water to warm.

He found a bottle of shampoo and sniffed
at it, recognizing the citrusy scent from Mia's
hair. Her body wash smelled like her, too, but he
didn't have any choice in the matter. "I'm going
to smell like a girl," he murmured.

When he was finished, Jack shut off the water,
then pushed the curtain back, only to find Mia,
sitting perched on the closed toilet seat, her legs
pulled up to her chest. "Did you change your
mind?" he asked.

Mia shook her head. "No, I'll jump in after
we have something to eat."

"Did you need to use the bathroom?"

She frowned, then watched as he grabbed a towel and dried himself. He'd known Mia for three days, seventy-two hours, and yet it seemed as if it had been so much longer.

"I—I just wanted to tell you that it doesn't have to be temporary," she said in a quiet voice. "Not that it can't be if that's what we choose. But I'm not— I just don't—" She drew a deep breath. "Whatever happens, happens. That's what I wanted to say."

Jack wrapped the towel around his waist and stepped out of the tub. He crossed the bathroom and stood in front of her, then reached out to cup her cheek in his hand. "I think that's a good decision, Mia," he said. "I don't like to operate with a lot of rules."

"Just promise me that it's not going to hurt," she said, leaning into his body. Mia pressed her lips against his damp chest and he wrapped his arms around her, pulling her close.

"It already hurts," he said. "You're an ache deep inside of me, Mia. I can't stop thinking about you, or wanting to touch you. And I'm not sure that feeling is going to go away anytime soon, no matter how far apart we are."

"I don't want to want you," she said. "I'm trying so hard not to, but I don't think it's working."

He brushed a kiss across her lips. "It's a mystery," Jack said. "No one can predict who they'll fall in love with. Or how long it will take. Or when it will happen. I think the best you can hope for is that you'll recognize it when it does come along."

She looked up at him and smiled. "I really don't know what I'm doing. You know, that whole friends-with-benefits thing could be a complete load of crap."

Jack nodded. "Yeah, I've been kind of thinking the same thing. A colossal load of crap." He hugged her, then pressed a kiss to the top of her head. "I'm glad we got that settled."

Mia slowly drew back. "Did you use my shampoo?"

"And your body wash."

"You smell like a girl," she said with a giggle. "I can lend you a pair of my underwear if you like."

"Now that would be sexy." He reached down and twisted his fingers in the hem of her dress, then slowly slid it over her head. Jack buried his face in the curve of her neck. "I kind of like the way you smell. At least I can find you in a dark closet."

Mia reached over and flipped off the light switch. "Is that better?"

Jack finished removing her underwear in the darkness. He never tired of touching her, of running his palms over her silken skin and soft flesh. If he walked away tomorrow, how long would it take for him to forget this wonderful sense of intimacy? He felt as if he'd known her forever and yet they were still strangers.

Was this what it took to make a relationship work? he wondered. This crazy state of limbo where he couldn't tell up from down, right from left, love from lust? With Mia, he lived in the moment and yet, he was certain that all their moments together would never be enough.

"Do we really need to go to this dance?" he murmured. "Couldn't we stay here and do our dancing in private?"

"You said you didn't know how to dance," Mia countered.

"My mom, my sisters and I used to dance around the living room on Saturday nights. She'd put on some Tony Bennett and get all misty-eyed." He slipped his arm around her waist and drew her close. "Let's give it a try. See if I remember."

Mia giggled. "We don't have any music," she said. "And we're naked in my bathroom."

"Hey, I'm not even sure I can dance. Adding music and clothing would just confuse the situation." He held up his right hand.

"I think you're supposed to lead, not me," she said.

"I knew that didn't feel right." He switched his

hands around and then nodded. "All right. Now what? I can't remember how to start."

"We just start moving," she said. "Come on, Fred Astaire, show me some moves."

He took a step to the left and they began to clumsily move around the bathroom. Every now and then, he'd shift unexpectedly and she'd step on his toes. But after a few minutes, he seemed to get the hang of it and there weren't any further injuries.

"See, that's not so bad. You could probably get through a dance at the Bellingham if we stick to the slow songs."

"Let's try a twirl," he said.

Mia stepped under his arm and he smoothly pulled her back into his embrace without losing a step. "It's all coming back to me now," he said. "Like riding a bike. Another?"

Mia nodded and a few seconds later, he twirled her twice. When he drew her back against his body, he pulled her closer, until their hips were touching.

"Let's try a dip," he whispered. Jack drew her leg up against his hip. His shaft was hard already and when it slipped between her legs, he heard her breath catch in her throat.

"And this is why they don't hold dances in bathrooms with naked people," she said, her hand drifting down his belly. "There's not even enough room for the band." When her fingers wrapped around his erection, Jack groaned.

"Maybe we should try it with music," Jack whispered, bending closer.

He could feel her breath on his lips, could sense that she was teetering on the edge of surrender. Mia ran her hand along his shoulder until her fingers tangled in the wet hair at his nape.

She sank against his body and drew him even closer. When their lips were nearly touching again, she smiled. "Maybe we can go to the bedroom. There's much more room for dancing there."

His gaze searched her face for a long moment and then he nodded before accepting her invitation. When their lips met, it was as if a switch had been thrown. A powerful current raced through his body and Jack moaned softly as he gathered her in his embrace.

They were still moving, almost dancing, as they stumbled down the hall to her bedroom. And when they fell onto the bed, Jack pulled Mia back into a long and desperate kiss. There was no going back for him. This woman had become the most important thing in his life and he had no intention of giving her up any time soon.

THE BELLINGHAM WAS a beautiful old hotel, built in the late thirties and once home to celebrities and movie stars visiting the city. The hotel had hosted Sunday–night big band dances for almost fifty years in their Crystal Ballroom, a glass-enclosed hall on the roof of the hotel. The dances had become a popular after-dinner destination for those who knew the difference between a foxtrot and a quick step.

Mia and Jack arrived an hour later than they planned, but Ben and Elyse were on the dance floor and didn't seem to notice. Elyse kissed Jack on the cheek and gave Mia a hug, then pointed to the table they'd reserved next to the dance floor. Jack took Mia's hand and led her off the floor, then pulled out her chair for her as she sat down.

Mia stared out at the dance floor, watching her father's graceful movements with Jack's mother in his arms. She remembered the parties in the gazebo, watching her parents and wondering if she'd ever be so in love with a man that she'd want to spend her life with him.

How did one ever recover from the loss of such perfect happiness? She drew a ragged breath and looked away, unable to watch as her father turned his attention to another woman.

"It's easier if you don't watch," Jack murmured, reaching out to take her hand.

"I'm being childish. I know it, but I can't help how I feel. I don't care if your mother is a wonderful person. It still hurts to see him moving on."

Jack stood up and held out his hand. "Come on, let's at least attempt to dance. Maybe it will take your mind off your misery."

Reluctantly, she took his hand and he led her out to the floor. He drew her into his arms and they moved along to the rhythm of the band. He was right. Being in his arms on the dance floor was a distraction. But how long would they be required to stay? Hell, she wasn't even sure why they'd been invited.

Mia rested her head on Jack's shoulder as she stared out at the dance floor, watching the graceful couples gliding along to the music, and the swirling lights creating patterns on the wood floor.

"How am I doing?" Jack asked.

She drew back and smiled. "Good," she said. "You're a pretty good dancer."

"I had a good teacher," he said.

"I think you probably learned more from your mother and Tony Bennett than you did from me in my bathroom."

He smoothed his hand gently over the small of her back, bending close until his forehead was pressed against hers. "Maybe you could just focus on all the good that came from our parents meeting."

"I guess you're right. If it weren't for them, there wouldn't be any us."

"Well, not necessarily. When I first saw you in the airport, I knew I had to meet you. I walked out and then I turned around and came back in looking for you. I was going to ask you out for a drink."

"Really? It wasn't because your name was on my sign?"

"Nope. Although, when I saw my name on your sign, I was pretty pleased. After all, it did make things a little easier. So, the way I see it, we would have probably ended up here, with or without our parents."

She smiled to herself. No matter what silly worries were going on in her head, Jack always managed to make her feel better about herself. He knew exactly the right thing to say to brighten her mood.

"All right," Mia murmured. "No more worrying over things I can't possibly change. You and I are going to have some fun."

They moved slowly into the next dance, a faster number that required a bit more focus on their footwork. But Jack gamely tried to follow and his attempts were more than amusing. By the time the song ended, they were laughing so hard that they could barely stand up straight.

"I need a drink," Jack said. "And I think your toes could use a break."

They walked back to the table and were surprised to find a bottle of champagne waiting in an ice bucket beside the table. Jack pulled it out and poured a glass for them both, then touched his glass to hers. "To us," he murmured.

Mia felt her heart skip a beat. "To us," she repeated.

As they sipped their champagne, they continued to watch the dancers. When the band's version of "I Left My Heart In San Francisco" ended, the band leader stepped to the microphone.

"Ladies and gentlemen, tonight is a special night here at the Bellingham. We have a couple here who first met fifty-five years ago. Their lives moved in separate directions, but through the wonder of modern technology, they met again about six months ago. We'd like to play this next song for Ben McMahon and Elyse Quinn."

Mia glanced over at Jack and forced a smile. "How sweet," she murmured.

But before the band could start the next number, her father stepped up onto the stage. "Ladies and gentlemen, I'm hoping you can give me a hand here. I've got a very important question to ask Elyse Quinn and I figure, what better opportunity will I have? Elyse, when you walked back into my life, everything changed. The happiness I thought I'd lost had returned. In your smile, in your sweet voice, in that beautiful face that hasn't changed in fifty years. Elyse, I can't imagine spending a minute away from you. Will you marry me?"

"What?" Mia cried.

"Oh, shit," Jack muttered.

"Yes!" Elyse said, her hands clasped to her chest.

"Yes?" Mia cried.

"No," Jack said.

They watched as Ben rushed down the steps and pulled Elyse into his arms. The room erupted into applause, as people gathered around the pair to congratulate them. Adding to the mood, the band began to play "Moon River." Ben pulled Elyse into his arms and led her around the dance floor, their gazes locked, tears glittering in Elyse's eyes.

Mia pressed her hand to her chest and felt her own tears threatening. She swallowed them back, knowing that once she started crying, she wouldn't be able to stop. Her dad hadn't even bothered to mention this to her, to ask how she and her sisters felt about him remarrying.

Oh, God, Elyse Quinn had managed to cast her spell in three short days. She'd probably been planning this all along, drawing him in for six months with letters and phone calls, knowing that as soon as he saw her, he'd be completely lost. "I have to go," Mia said, her voice thick and barely audible.

"Mia, come on. You can't. We have to at least say something to them."

"You said she didn't want to get married again. You said she'd never leave Chicago."

"Maybe she isn't going to," Jack said.

Mia groaned. She grabbed her purse and started toward the door, but Jack caught her and pulled her back to the table. "Stop," he said. "You're not going to run away from this. We're going to offer them our best wishes and then we can leave."

"No," Mia said. "This is crazy. They've known each other for three days. What do you think they'd say if we announced our engagement after just three days? Do you think they'd be happy about that? No! They'd be doing everything they could to convince us that we didn't belong together."

"Look, they're heading over here," Jack said. "You're going to smile and congratulate them and then you and I are going to get the hell out of here and find ourselves something stronger to drink."

When Ben and Elyse arrived at the table, Mia steeled her emotions and pasted a smile on her face. She gave Elyse the perfunctory kiss and lied through her teeth about looking forward to having her in the family. Jack probably did the same, though Mia's head was buzzing so loudly that she could barely hear herself speak.

When it was over, Jack took her hand and led her out of the ballroom. They got into the elevator and rode down twenty floors to the lobby, Mia biting on her bottom lip in an attempt to keep herself from weeping.

They waited out front for the valet to bring her car and when it arrived, Jack helped her into the passenger side and took his place behind the wheel. The moment he got inside, Mia clenched her fists and screamed as loud as she could. She pounded on the dashboard and kicked her feet, the tantrum loud enough to draw the attention of the parking valets.

"Go!" she shouted.

Jack pulled the car out onto the street and aimlessly drove toward the bay. Mia stared out the window, shaking her head. "What are we going to do?"

"I don't know," Jack said. "I don't think we can have them committed. Maybe you and your sisters could make up some kind of emergency to get him out of town. Or maybe my sisters would do that."

"Would they?"

"Probably not. They were thrilled when my

mother reconnected with your dad. They won't be any help at all."

"My sisters are a different story," Mia said. "I need to call them. They'll know exactly what to do."

Jack pulled the car over to the curb and turned to Mia. "Are you sure you want to do this, Mia? You understand that you might be ruining your father's happiness?"

"He's not thinking straight," Mia insisted. "You don't make a decision like this after just three days. No one falls in love in three days."

Jack turned away and stared out the windshield. "I don't know. I never thought it was possible, but now, I'm not so sure."

Mia groaned, shaking her head. "Just take me home."

MIA WAS CURLED UP ON her bed, still wearing the pretty flowered dress she'd chosen for the Bellingham dance. She'd kicked off her bright pink shoes and they were sitting on the floor beside the bed.

Jack sat down next to her and held out the mug of tea. "Drink it," he said. "It will make you feel better."

The minute they'd gotten back to her apartment, she'd crawled into bed and refused to speak, staring at the wall without registering any emotion whatsoever. Jack would have preferred it if she'd shouted or cursed or wept uncontrollably. At least then he'd know what she was thinking. But the silence was difficult to interpret.

"You're going to have to talk to me sooner or later, Mia."

"It's not that I don't want to talk to you," she said.

"Do you blame me for this?"

"No!" She sat up and crossed her legs in front of her, then took the mug from his hand. For a long moment, she stared down at the tea, as if she was trying to formulate an explanation for her behavior. She opened her mouth once to speak, then snapped it shut and shook her head.

Suddenly, her eyes began to fill with tears. Huge, watery droplets tumbled down her cheeks and landed in her lap. Jack leaned close and pulled her into his embrace. "Oh, sweetheart, don't cry. It's going to be all right. I swear it will."

"No, it won't," she said, her voice cracking. "I'm a terrible, terrible daughter. He's never going to forgive me for running out like that. He just wanted me to be happy for him and I couldn't do it. I couldn't allow him that much."

Jack drew back and looked into her face, wondering at the change in her attitude. "I'm sure he's not thinking that."

"It just happened so fast," she said. "Didn't you think it was fast? Too fast?"

"Yeah. But I guess when you're their age, you don't want to waste another day."

"Do you believe people can fall in love in three days?" Mia asked.

That was the million dollar question. And the only way he could answer was with the truth, as improbable as it seemed. "I do," Jack admitted. "Look at us, at how quickly things have happened between us. We didn't really think about what we were doing. We just acted. It may not be love, but it's a powerful thing. And maybe that's what's happening with your father."

"You think he might be making a mistake?"

"I think he might have been swept away by the moment," Jack said. "And my mother might have gotten swept away with him. Maybe they'll realize it later. Or maybe not."

"That's a lot of maybes," Mia muttered. "You sound like someone who really isn't sure about anything."

"Well, you'd be right there."

She sat back in bed, sinking into the pillows stacked against the headboard of the bed, then took a slow sip of the tea. Jack watched as she evaluated his explanation. But she couldn't know that his feelings were more than just superficial. He didn't just believe that a man could fall in love in three days. Jack was actually experiencing it for himself.

The notion had seemed impossible at first, but the more he thought about it, the more Jack believed that what he was feeling for Mia was love. There was no other explanation. When he thought about leaving her and going home, he felt an ache in his heart so deep that he could barely breathe. He'd spent the past few days trying to figure out a way to make a relationship work and had come to the conclusion that the only sensible thing was to take the new job in California and give it a go.

Though he changed his mind five or six times every hour, he knew that by the end of the week, he'd have to have something figured out. He didn't care if Mia wasn't ready to admit her own feelings for him. Jack was willing to wait. For Mia, he would wait as long as it took for her to recognize what they shared.

"It seems like only yesterday," Mia said softly. "But it's been three years."

"I barely remember my dad. I was nine when he died. Sometimes, I look at a photo of him and he's like a stranger to me. But other times, I have these dreams and we're talking to each other and it's like I remember everything about him."

"That's so young to lose a parent," Mia said.

"I have photos of him teaching me how to ride

a bike and throw a football, but I don't remember the actual events."

"I don't want to forget her," Mia said. "And I don't want my father to, either."

A long silence grew between them and Jack stared down into her beautiful face. He knew her so intimately already, yet he hadn't a clue about her childhood. "Tell me about her," he murmured.

Over the next hour, she talked, telling him everything about her parents, her sisters, the life she'd led before he'd met her. Jack settled in beside her and listened, knowing that everything she told him would add to his own picture of the woman she was. He didn't ask questions or interrupt, he just allowed her to offload all her thoughts.

"I was kind of a tomboy as a kid," Mia said. "My dad didn't have any sons, so by the time my mom had me, he decided, if I was a girl, he was going to treat me like his son. My sisters were into boys and makeup, while I played tennis and swam. I was always trying to please my dad, but in high school, I realized that the person I really wanted to please was my mom. She had such a quiet confidence and I wanted to be just like her."

"She sounds like a remarkable woman," Jack said.

Just the chance to talk had already calmed

Mia's troubled mind. Jack could feel her relaxing beside him, stretching out tense limbs until they were soft and supple, her leg tossed over his hips, her arm resting across his chest.

"We should probably drive back to the house in the morning," Jack said. "Just to make sure everything is all right."

"I can apologize then," Mia said. She drew a deep breath. "I feel much better now. The tea really helped. But I'm starving."

"I could eat," Jack said. "Are you going to cook for me?"

"No," Mia said. She rolled over and opened the drawer of her bedside table, then pulled out a stack of crumpled menus, setting them down in front of him. "I'll let you pick the restaurant. Thai Palace delivers, so does Donatello's Pizza and Spiros Greek. The King of Szechuan has the best General Tso's chicken in the world and if you like barbeque, I'd recommend Larry's. Other than that, I have bread and cheese in the fridge. If you'd like, I could make you a really good grilled cheese sandwich," she said.

"Add some tomato soup and you've got my favorite meal," Jack said.

"I think I have tomato soup," Mia said.

Jack smiled, then leaned closer and brushed a kiss across her lips. Her soft hair tickled his cheek and he drew a deep breath and kissed her again, this time with more purpose.

It was impossible to be close to her without touching her and when she wrapped her arms around his neck, Jack pulled her close, dragging her beneath him.

His fingers tangled in her hair and her body grew soft and pliant to his touch. She wasn't a perfect woman, he'd come to realize. But that didn't matter. She was perfect for him.

Jack gently stretched out beside her. His hands skimmed over her body, searching for a place to rest. When he found her waist, Jack pulled her on top of him, dragging her thighs up along his hips. The friction between them was enough to send a jolt of desire racing through him and he arched against her, his pleasure frustrated by the clothing they still wore.

He felt himself growing hard and he wanted to stop, to slow down. But she was just too much. Just the taste of her was enough to send his senses into overdrive. When her fingers fumbled with the buttons of his shirt, he watched her silently.

Once the fabric was parted, Mia slipped her hands beneath his shirt and ran her palms over his chest. Jack's heart slammed in a rapid rhythm. He'd always been so cool and composed when it came to seducing women, but with Mia, he'd lost all sense of control.

Her lips found the warm pulse beneath his ear. Jack wanted to tell her then, to whisper the words, to make his feelings for her clear. He drew a breath and then another, but he knew what saying the words might cost him. Mia didn't believe that what they shared was anything more than just passion. But Jack knew it ran deeper.

For now, the feelings would have to remain his own.

# 6

MONDAY MORNING BROUGHT rain and fog. Mia woke to the sound of the hiss of raindrops outside her bedroom window. She reached out to grab her alarm clock, but when Jack felt her move, he hugged her body closer to his, pulling her backside into his lap and pressing a kiss to her shoulder.

"What time is it?" he mumbled.

Mia squinted to make out the alarm clock through her sleepy eyes. "I think it's eight-thirty." She flopped back down on the pillow.

"Just give me an hour. Two tops. That's all I need."

They'd stayed up late last night, talking and making love, then talking a little more. It was wonderful to have the freedom to spend the entire night together. And it was even more incredible to have a man in her bed.

Mia smiled to herself. Though she'd set out to have a no-strings affair, she knew they were already completely tangled up in each other's lives. He'd be going back to Chicago before the end of the week and by that time, Mia knew there would be no easy way to say goodbye.

Though long-distance relationships were difficult, Jack had mentioned a job offer in L.A., which would at least put him on the West Coast. It was a start, a way that they.could see if this short-term arrangement might thrive in the long run.

Mia rolled over and faced him. His hair was mussed and his faced shadowed by the scruff of a beard. Reaching out, she smoothed her hand over his cheek and Jack opened his eyes.

"Don't start anything with me," he warned. "I need more sleep."

"I'm not starting anything," she said. "What do you eat for breakfast?"

"Coffee," he said. "And whatever fast-food breakfast sandwich I can put my hands on. I also require a newspaper with the box scores from yesterday's games. The Cubs played last night."

"There's a newspaper on the porch downstairs," Mia said. "Of course, you'll have to get to it before my downstairs neighbor steals it. And I have coffee. We'll need to go out for the rest, though."

"Do we have to get up now? Can't we stay in bed a little longer?"

"You'll have to get the paper now," she said. "The rest can wait."

Groaning, Jack rolled out of bed. "Do I need to put on clothes to grab the paper?"

Mia giggled. "At least put on your underwear. That way, if you get locked out, you won't get arrested for public nudity. Or propositioned by my neighbor, Mrs. Beauchamp. She adores younger men. In fact, she actually used to *be* a younger man."

"I love San Francisco," Jack said. He searched around until he found his khakis, then tugged them on, leaving the top button undone. Mia listened to his footsteps on the stairs as he walked down the three flights to the street level. A few seconds later, the buzzer for the front door rang and she shook her head.

Tugging a T-shirt over her head, Mia scrambled out of bed and hurried to the open front door to buzz him back in. But a few moments later, Jack walked back into the apartment... followed by her father.

Mia gasped. "Daddy! What are you doing here?"

"I came to talk to you about last night," Ben said. "I didn't expect that you'd have company."

She glanced over at Jack. From the way he

was dressed—or not dressed—it was pretty clear what was going on between them. Should she go with the truth or would it be worth it to try to convince her father that he'd slept on the sofa?

"Yes," she said. "Jack spent the night."

"You know, why don't I go out and get us all some coffee. I'll just grab my shoes and a shirt and get out of your way."

"I think that would be best," Ben said, fixing a dismissive gaze in Jack's direction.

Mia held her breath as Jack hurried to the bedroom. A few seconds later, he came out, carrying his shoes and a shirt. He smiled at her as he slipped out the door and Mia drew another breath.

"What the hell are you doing, Mia? Are you sleeping with him?"

"Yes," she said. "But it's nothing serious. We're not going to get married any time soon."

"Is that supposed to make me feel better?"

"I'm sorry, Daddy, but I'm an adult now and I can make these decisions for myself. So, if you've come here to lecture me on the sad state of my morals, you can turn around and go home. I'm not interested in listening."

"That's not why I came," Ben said. "I wanted to talk to you about last night. You seemed upset when you left."

Mia stared at him for a long moment. "You

think? Daddy, you announced your engagement in front of a hundred strangers, to a woman you've known three days. Don't you think you could have at least clued me in a little bit before you popped the big question?"

"I wasn't sure I was going to do it any earlier," Ben said.

Mia sat down on the sofa and patted the place beside her. Ben ignored the invitation and began to pace on the other side of the coffee table. "This is not going to change anything between you and me."

"But it's going to change everything, Daddy. You're moving on. But your three daughters can't. I just can't see you with anyone but Mom. It's only been three years."

"Three years seems like an eternity. Believe me, Mimi, I never thought I'd find someone who'd be interested in spending her life with me. But I did. And I hope to God I don't lose her the way I lost your mother."

"It feels like a betrayal to me," Mia said.

"Oh, honey, no." Ben shook his head. "Your mother and I had many discussions about this, the year before she died. She convinced me that I needed to move on if she ever left me. And for three years I tried, I really did. Then Elyse appeared and I thought, here's a woman who might be exactly what I'm looking for."

"Where are you going to live?"

"I don't know yet. Elyse and I haven't discussed it. Probably California, but I'm sure we'll spend a few months a year in Chicago to be close to her family."

"You seem to have all the answers, Daddy," Mia said, slowly standing.

Ben reached out and grasped her shoulders. "Mia, I need you and your sisters to understand. This woman can make me happy. And I can make her happy, too. She isn't my one and only. That was your mother. And for Elyse, it was her husband. But together, we make a pretty good pair and I want to make sure she's in my life for however long that lasts."

Mia drew a deep breath. It wasn't her decision to make, nor was it her sisters'. Though she'd worried over her father for the past three years, it was time for both of them to move forward. He'd get a new wife and she'd get…she'd get her life back.

"I understand," she said.

Her father pulled her into a fierce hug, then stepped back and looked down into her eyes. "Thank you, Mimi. You don't know how happy you've made me." He rubbed his hands together. "I have to go. Elyse is waiting back at the house. We're going to drive up the coast and look at a few venues for the wedding. It's going to be very small. Just close family and a few friends."

Mia pasted a smile on her face. Though she could accept Elyse's presence in her life, she was not going to comment on her wedding plans. "I'm sure it will be lovely."

Ben kissed her cheek and walked to the door. He paused, then turned around. "I don't like this thing with Jack," he said. "But we'll talk about that another time."

He closed the door behind him and Mia lowered herself onto the sofa, then covered her eyes with her hands. This was all too much to take in, especially on about three hours of sleep. Mia wandered back into the bedroom and tugged the T-shirt over her head.

Crawling back under the covers, she found the sheets still warm. Mia pulled the covers up over her head and pinched her eyes closed. When she was little and she was confused by the world, an hour or two under the covers always helped. But now that she was older, she had other ways to cope.

She and Jack would figure this all out and find a way to make it work for both families. She could trust Jack to know what to do. He would make things better.

JACK WASN'T SURE HOW long he ought to give Mia and her father, but the last thing he wanted was to get in the middle of a family argument. Then again, since he was probably the cause of that argument, he should have stuck around to help her out.

"Coward," he muttered.

Actually, he was afraid he might say or do something stupid. What could you say to a guy who capriciously threw marriage proposals around as if they were cheap confetti? Jack's mother deserved more than some fickle suitor who'd probably change his mind once the going got tough.

Still, Jack couldn't help but feel a little sorry for the guy. The man had lost the love of his life three years ago. How did someone ever deal with that? Maybe Ben was just desperate to find something as powerful and enduring as he'd had with Mia's mother. And Jack's mom just got caught in the cross fire.

Fifteen minutes had been long enough for Jack to grab three coffees from a nearby Starbucks and head back to Mia's flat. But he didn't want to interrupt a private discussion, so he decided to give them a half hour. He found a place on a park bench across the street and sipped at his coffee, watching the front door of Mia's flat. After forty-five minutes, he gathered his resolve, walked across the street and rang her bell. If the argument wasn't over yet, maybe he could offer a bit of help.

The door lock buzzed and he stepped inside and made the long trek up the three flights of stairs. She was waiting for him at the top, dressed in the same way he'd left her, in just an oversize T-shirt, her legs bare.

"Is he still here?" Jack whispered.

Mia shook her head and winced. "Dad only stayed a few minutes. He was pretty upset. It probably wasn't the best way to start the day."

"Oh, Mia, I'm sorry. I just opened the door to get the paper and there he was."

She shrugged carelessly. "I don't care. If he can spontaneously ask a woman to marry him after just three days, I can certainly sleep with that woman's son if I want to. There's really no difference. On a scale of recklessness, we're both pushing the envelope."

Jack frowned. That she tried to make an equivalency of their situations was a bit irrational. Even through the flip attitude, he could see Mia was upset. Was she upset enough to put Jack out of her life just to please her father?

Jack handed her a coffee and they walked back into the bedroom and sat down on the bed. Mia crossed her legs in front of her and braced her elbows on her knees, watching him as he kicked off his shoes.

"He's always treated me like a child," she explained. "My older sisters married young and Daddy was so happy that they found husbands who could look after them. It was as if he thought they were unable to survive on their own. He's always wanted me to get married, and of course, he wants me to choose someone exactly like my two brothers-in-law. They're both bankers. Oh, and boring. Unimaginative. Very uptight."

"Not your type?" Jack asked.

"Not even close. I told him I want someone exciting. Someone who wants more than a house in the suburbs, a country club membership and a vacation in Cancun once a year."

"Someone like me," Jack said, sending her a grin.

"Yes! Exactly!" She looked at him and an instant later, she realized what she'd said. Jack watched as her cheeks turned pink with embarrassment. "Not that I expect you to marry me. We've only known each other three days."

"Going on four," he said. "But don't panic— no one gets married after only four days."

"Aren't our parents supposed to be the ones with all the good sense? Four days and they're driving up the coast to look at wedding venues. Just so you know, it's going to be a small wedding, with just family and friends."

"What?" Jack gasped, shaking his head. "Really? It's gone that far already?"

"Yes. They're not only engaged, they're planning on getting married right away."

Jack sighed deeply, tipping his head back and closing his eyes. "I need to talk to her. This is not like my mother at all. She is always so careful about making decisions. And this is obviously a bad one."

"You don't think they'll be happy?" Mia asked.

Jack cursed softly. The truth was, he'd hoped his mother would find happiness in a new marriage. But he'd always thought she'd find someone in Chicago, someone who'd be familiar to the family before any wedding plans were announced. Someone he could thoroughly investigate before any promises were made. He didn't know anything about what Ben McMahon expected from a wife.

"My mother is very independent. She doesn't really like anyone telling her what to do."

"She sounds like me," Mia said. "And you see how me and my father get on lately."

Jack cursed again. "You know what? I'm tired of worrying about our parents. I think you should spend the day showing me San Francisco. I've never ridden one of those trolley cars. I've never been to Chinatown. We need to let them make their own mistakes."

Mia reached out and grabbed his hand, pulling it to her chest. "All right," she said. "Today, it's just you and me. We'll see the city and then maybe catch a movie this afternoon. Then we'll hit Chinatown for dinner. We won't even think about my dad and your mom. They're certainly not thinking about us right now."

"And tomorrow, I'm going to fly down to L.A. and talk to SportsNet about that job. I'd like you to come with me. They're going to put me up in a swanky hotel and pay for all my expenses. We could have a nice time." He wagged his eyebrows at her.

"I have a few clients I could see," she hedged.

"Perfect. I'll have the network make flight arrangements for two and we'll leave tomorrow afternoon."

He had barely thought of the job at Sports-Net USA since he'd been approached a year ago. There had been no reason to make such a big change in his life. But with his mother remarrying, Jack suddenly had a chance to reboot his life and maybe find a way to include Mia in it. He was no longer tied to Chicago.

It wouldn't hurt to live on the West Coast. Weekends together would be much easier. And maybe he could work out of San Francisco for part of the week. Jack crawled over the bed and settled in next to Mia. "We're going to have to go back to your dad's place to pick up the rest of my stuff."

Mia chuckled. "After this morning, I don't think he's going to be too happy to see you. Thank God you didn't go down in your underwear. That would have been embarrassing."

"And I really should talk to my mom."

"My sisters are going to be livid," Mia said.

"And my sisters are going to be hysterical," Jack countered.

"They'd be better off running away to Vegas. If they have the wedding here, the 'anyone objects' part of the ceremony is going to be a disaster."

He reached out and took her hand, pressing a kiss to the center of her palm. "There is one good thing that can come from this. I really don't have anything keeping me in Chicago now. I can consider the job in L.A."

"So you can be closer to your mom?"

Jack shook his head. "No, Mia. So I can be closer to you."

"Me?"

"I'm thinking we should reconsider our arrangement. I don't want you to use me just for sex anymore."

"What should I use you for?"

"I could take you out to dinner occasionally. We could go to ball games or on hikes. I could drive you to the airport when you need to go, or paint your kitchen when you want a change. Heck, we could even go shopping." He gave a mock shiver.

Mia gave him a coy look, a tiny smile twitching at the corners of her mouth. "So you want to be my…personal assistant?"

"Yeah, that, too," Jack said with a chuckle. "Personally, I think we should spend every minute we can together. We should make plans and get to know each other better and think about the future and—"

Mia leaned close and kissed him, her lips soft and damp against his. "Slow down," she said. "Maybe you should see if you really want this job and then we can decide what to do?"

"All right. I can live with that. Job first, then the girl."

She curled up beside him, resting her head on his chest. "You know, this could be really strange. If our parents are married, then I'm going to be dating my stepbrother."

"We could always get married first and then our parents would be the ones feeling weird."

Mia giggled. "Oh, very funny. You're sounding as crazy as my father."

"You didn't know that about me?" Jack asked. "I'm a funny and crazy guy."

She smoothed her hand over his chest in a lazy motion. "What else don't I know about you?"

"Where do I start?" Jack cleared his throat. "Well, I think baseball is the greatest game ever. I think there are mysteries of life buried deep in the sport. I've never seen a no-hitter, but I came close. And if I could do anything in the world, I'd play shortstop for the 1932 Cubs so I could have seen Ruth call his home run."

"So you kind of like baseball, huh?" Mia teased.

He nodded. "What do you like, Mia McMahon?"

Mia thought for a long moment. "Strawberry ice cream. The sound of birds singing in the morning. Roasted marshmallows. Christmas Eve. And flannel pajamas on a chilly night."

"What's your opinion on pizza with pineapple?"

"It's sacrilegious," she said. "Anchovies?"

"Never," Jack said. "Thick or thin crust?"

"Thin. Always thin."

Jack frowned, shaking his head slowly. "We're going to have to work on that one. I'm not sure if we'll be able to overcome our differences."

"I guess we're doomed," Mia said. "I should

let you know that I like Chinese food more than pizza, anyway."

This time Jack groaned, covering his face with his hands. "Oh, that's not good at all."

Mia leaned over him. "But I am really, really good at kissing guys. In fact, I'm considered a bit of a savant in that area. My talents are quite extraordinary."

Pushing up on his elbows, Jack's interest was suddenly piqued. It was a silly game they were playing, but it was fun. He wanted to know more. "Well, that might mitigate some of our problems. But I'd have to know exactly what you mean." His gaze fixed on her lips. At that moment, nothing mattered but the two of them.

He dropped a kiss on her mouth. "See, this is important. We're learning things here," Jack said.

"I don't like liars. Promise me you'll never lie to me. I can handle the truth. If you find someone else, if you decide we don't belong together, just say it. Promise me we'll always be completely honest with each other."

Jack wasn't sure he could make that promise. If he knew one thing, he knew that he could never do anything to hurt Mia. And sometimes complete and total honesty could hurt. Still, part of his problem with Melanie had been that they never really told each other how they were feeling. By the time their relationship was over, Jack wasn't even sure when they'd stopped loving each other.

"I will promise you that. I will always tell you the truth, Mia."

"All right," she said. "And I'll tell you the truth, too."

"I think that's a good place to start."

Jack pulled her into his embrace and hugged her. "Why don't we take a shower and then find some lunch. We can go see our parents tomorrow morning before we head out to L.A. Today should be just for us."

Mia got up on her knees beside him, pushing her tangled hair out of her eyes. "If we go out, you can't wear that T-shirt. It looks like it's been used to wash the kitchen floor. I'm just being honest. I think maybe you should take it off right now. And those pants are horrible. They barely fit you. They need to go, too. Just being honest."

At first Jack didn't know what she was talking about, then he saw the teasing glint in her eyes. "Well, as long as we're going there, that T-shirt of yours is obnoxiously ugly."

As they discarded the offending garments, Jack realized that he didn't care if they ever left her apartment. He'd be perfectly happy to live in her bed for the rest of his life. He was seriously hooked on this woman and there wasn't a thing he wanted to do about it.

AFTER A MORNING SPENT in Mia's bed, she and Jack spent the afternoon walking around the city, exploring all of Mia's favorite spots. She was continually amazed at how easy things were with Jack. He was so even-tempered that they rarely had any disagreements. And those they did have were minor and easily resolved with a joke or a kiss.

Mia had been involved with other men in the past, but she'd never felt this kind of connection. When she was with Jack, she was a better version of herself—she was optimistic, calm and centered. She knew exactly who she was and what she wanted and she wasn't afraid to ask for it.

As they walked up the hill toward her flat, Jack chatted about their trip to Los Angeles. They'd leave tomorrow afternoon, since his meeting was scheduled for the next day. Mia had thought about how her life would change if he moved to the West Coast, but she was also careful not to get too invested until he was actually offered the job.

Though they wouldn't live in the same city, they would be much closer geographically. Long-distance relationships were almost impossible to keep going, but in this case, the distance would be a short one. It would give her enough time and space to make the adjustments needed, but wouldn't require too many hours apart.

"I like this city," Jack said. "Except for the earthquakes. I've never been in an earthquake."

"There was one this morning," she said. "Just a small one. Right before we got in the shower. The earth actually moved. Didn't you feel it?"

"Yeah? I'm not talking about those kind of earthquakes. I'm talking about the ones where all the buildings fall down on top of me."

"Yeah, those are kind of scary. But I always think it's a trade-off for living in the most beautiful city in the world. There's no place that's perfect. Chicago is cold and windy in the winter."

As they approached Mia's flat, she noticed someone sitting on the front steps. She grabbed Jack's arm. "Is that your mom?" she asked.

Jack stopped short and squinted against the late-afternoon sun. "Yeah, I think it is."

He jogged down the sidewalk ahead of Mia and she watched as Elyse Quinn stood up and gave her son a hug. Mia joined them a few moments later and noticed that Elyse's eyes were red, as if she'd been crying. Two overnight bags sat on the sidewalk in front of her, the same two that Mia had helped unload from the trunk of her father's car that first day.

"Is everything all right?" Mia asked. "Did something happen?"

"Mia, maybe you could give us a minute," Jack said.

Elyse shook her head. "No. No, I'd like to talk to Mia. Jack, why don't you grab your bag and take it up to Mia's flat while I have a word with her."

Mia glanced over at Jack and he shrugged his shoulders, then did as he was asked. He grabbed his bag from the sidewalk and disappeared up the stairs.

"What are you doing here?" Mia asked. "Did my dad bring you?"

"Your father and I had a huge fight. I took a cab here."

Mia gasped. "A fight? About what? You barely know each other. How could you possibly find something to fight about?"

"Well, when you have children, that's not such a hard thing." She pointed to the front step. "Do you mind if we sit? This whole thing has me a bit worn out."

"No," Mia said. "Of course not."

Elyse sat next to Mia on the second step, then took a moment to gather her thoughts. "I know your father shocked you last night with his proposal. And I probably shocked you with my acceptance. It was all very romantic at the time.

But, it turns out we were just a little bit hasty about our plans."

"What happened?" Mia asked.

"We just weren't on the same page when it came to our children. And I guess, for both of us, that's a deal breaker."

Mia studied Elyse's expression but Jack's mother didn't betray a hint of anger or regret. Instead, she seemed almost resigned. "You argued over us? Me and Jack?"

"Your father felt Jack was taking advantage of you. And I know my son. He doesn't take relationships with women lightly. He doesn't trust easily, but if you can break down that wall around his heart, I know he can love so deeply that you'd never regret choosing him."

Mia drew in a deep breath and then let it out slowly. "My father worries about me. We've been through a lot together and I think he's concerned that I might not be able to weather another storm. He's just being protective. I'm sure he didn't mean to get angry with you. Or to disparage Jack in any way."

Elyse nodded slowly. "I understand his feelings about Jack. I happen to disagree. I think you're young and you should take chances, Mia. Trust your heart to find the way."

Emotion surged up inside of her and Mia felt tears threaten. "My mother always used to tell me that. Nothing ventured, nothing gained. She had all sorts of little sayings."

"I'm certain she was a very smart woman. She raised a smart daughter."

"I'm not that easy to get along with," Mia admitted. "I don't trust quickly. Sometimes, I keep people at a distance. But with Jack, I feel like the old Mia is gone. Maybe there's a new Mia inside of me."

"Well, I'm glad we got a chance to talk. I need to get to the airport and catch my flight back to Chicago, but I'm hoping that I'll see you there sometime in the future."

"I hope so, too." Mia slowly realized that.

Elyse spotted a cab coming up the street and she got up and hurried to the curb to wave it down. When it stopped, she turned back to Mia. "I had a wonderful time this weekend. And even though it didn't work out, I don't have any regrets. Because if it brought you and Jack together, then the trip served its purpose."

Mia stood and grabbed Elyse's bag, then carried it to the waiting cabbie. While the driver put it in the trunk, Mia gave Elyse a fierce hug. "He's not such a bad guy," she said softly.

"I'm glad you realize that," Elyse said.

Mia stepped back. "I meant my father."

"I know you did. Tell Jack to call me later tonight. I should be home before midnight if all goes well."

"Are you sure you don't want to talk to him?" Mia said. "He's probably upstairs pacing in my apartment."

"And have him start with all the I-told-you-so's? No, I think we'll leave those for later."

Elyse got into the cab and waved to Mia as they drove off down the hill toward the Esplanade. She smiled to herself as she thought about what Jack's mother had said. What a wonderful stepmother she would have made. There was no doubt she would have made a perfect wife for Mia's father.

"Oh, Daddy, how did you manage to mess this up?"

Mia turned for the front steps and climbed them, but before she got to the door, Jack burst out. "Where did she go? How could you let her leave?"

Mia held out her hand to calm him. "She went to the airport. She was hoping to catch a flight out."

He glanced up and down the street, then cursed softly. "Didn't she want to talk to me?"

"I think she was a little embarrassed by what happened," Mia explained.

"What did happen?"

Mia stepped up to Jack and slipped her arms

around his waist. "They had a fight. About us. My father must have said some things about you that your mother found unacceptable and they broke up."

A frown creased Jack's brow. "Our being together broke them up?" A slow smile filled his expression. "Isn't that what we wanted all along? As long as we're together, they'll be apart?"

"I think so," Mia replied.

"That was easy."

She pushed away from him and sat down on the front steps, wrapping her arms around her legs. "I think they might have actually been able to make each other happy. I'm sad that it didn't work out for them."

"Come on, Mia, you've been against it from the start."

"And now I'm not. And what about you? If your mother is still living in Chicago, why would you move to L.A.?"

He thought about her question for a long moment. "That's simple. Because you're here."

"You still want to move out here?"

Jack plopped down beside her. "Yeah. If you still want me."

Mia groaned, then wrapped her arms around his neck. "When have I ever not wanted you, Jack Quinn?"

# 7

THE BED IN THEIR Beverly Hills hotel room was massive with a mattress that seemed to go on forever and linens that were so soft on the skin, Jack couldn't wait to get naked.

He and Mia had arrived two hours before and had decided to lie down for a quick nap before they set out to find a place for dinner. But as always, they got distracted by carnal pleasures and eating was soon forgotten.

Jack stared down at Mia's body, her long limbs stretched out in front of him. She writhed beneath his touch, searching for that perfect caress that would bring on her orgasm. But Jack was in a teasing mood tonight and he planned to take his time in pleasuring her.

Nothing had prepared him for the intensity of his need for Mia. They were both completely caught in a riptide of desire and it sometimes threatened to swallow them both. Sex with her was a revelation, an experience that defined the two of them as a couple. What they couldn't express in words, they expressed in desire, leaving them both to realize that what they shared was deep and powerful.

Jack ran his hands over her naked body as she caressed him, her flesh warm and soft against his palms. Already, it was taking more willpower than he had to maintain control. He wanted to bury himself inside her, to feel her warmth surround him, but tonight was about anticipation.

Every moment they shared was a chance for him to get to know her better, to find out what secret desires she still kept hidden. Though they were almost strangers, there was an undeniable connection between them, as if they'd known each other for weeks and months instead of just days.

Jack drew Mia beneath him, then slowly began a careful exploration of her body with his lips. She arched as he moved down from her breast to her belly and then to a spot just above her hip. Everything about her aroused him, from the scent of her skin to the tiny beauty mark he discovered on her thigh.

Was there anything about her that he didn't find fascinating? Jack tried to remember the last time he'd wanted a woman as much as he wanted

Mia, but the effort to even recall his past lovers didn't seem worth the time. This woman was... everything.

Jack slid off the bed and gently kissed the insides of her thighs. He moved higher and when he found the damp spot between her legs, he flicked his tongue along the crease. Her body jerked in response, but he couldn't stop there. Gently, he began to tease her, waiting for each response and then using it to his advantage.

Her fingers clutched at his hair, pulling him forward and then pushing him away when the sensations became too much for her to bear. Jack sensed when she'd reached her limit but didn't want to stop. How far could he take her? He wanted her to surrender and yet he wanted to experience that delicious capitulation along with her.

He stretched out on the bed and nuzzled her neck, gently keeping her on the edge with his fingers. Mia stared at him through passion-glazed eyes. "Why is this always so good?" she whispered.

Jack growled softly. "I guess we're just the right fit."

She nodded, her lower lip caught between her teeth. "It just keeps getting better."

"We've had lots of time to practice."

She wrapped her arm around his head and

pulled him close. "I'm a very dedicated student." Her breath caught in her throat and she moaned softly.

Her body writhed beneath his touch and she reached out to wrap her fingers around his shaft. The moment she touched him, Jack realized that sleeping in separate beds the night before had only increased his craving for release. Every nerve in his body felt like it was on fire. He reached over and grabbed the box of condoms that he'd tossed onto the bed.

Mia took the packages from him and tore open one. As she sheathed him, Jack realized how close he was to the end of it all. Suddenly, he wanted to delay, to stop this headlong race toward satisfaction. How long would they have together? Would he be flying back home soon? He sighed softly as he settled between her legs.

He waited to enter her, marshalling his self-control and focusing on something other than her naked body.

"What's wrong?" Mia asked.

"I'm not sure I can wait," he said.

She wrapped her arms around his neck and laughed. "Why?"

Jack nuzzled his face into her neck. "I'm usually really good at this," he said. "Really. I can give you references. But you do something to me that makes it difficult to maintain control."

"Tell me what it is," she whispered. "I'll try to fix it."

He probed gently at her entrance, then slipped inside of her. The breath left his body. He moved slowly, burying himself inch by inch. He was good at this, Jack reminded himself. That was one thing he was sure of. When he was buried completely, he waited, knowing that it would take every ounce of his control to hold back and wait for her.

"I—I think you're doing—just fine," she replied with tiny gasps.

He moved, drawing back and then plunging a little deeper. Every thrust brought them to a new pinnacle of pleasure. He read her responses, her soft sighs and breathless pleas, the way her body reacted to their joining. And when she finally dissolved into uncontrollable spasms, it was all he could do to hold on for just a few more minutes. He became lost in a maelstrom of incredible sensation.

She was everything he'd hoped she'd be— passionate, uninhibited, responsive. With every kiss and every thrust, he felt as if they'd discovered something beautiful to share. This was new to him. The physical connection was undeniable, but there was something deeper at work. He just couldn't put words to it.

As the passion grew more intense between

them, self-awareness vanished and instinct took over. He focused only on the pleasure that each movement brought.

Grabbing her waist, he pulled her on top of him, anxious to watch her reaction to what they were experiencing. Mia's hair fell in unruly waves around her flushed face. Jack reached up and smoothed the strands back and she met his gaze. A lazy smile touched her lips and he had all the answers he needed.

When he reached between them and touched her, the contact startled her for a moment. And then she moaned softly and slowed her pace. Slowly, his caress transformed her, bringing Mia closer and closer to the edge. He'd never really paid attention to the pleasure he gave a woman. Usually, he was only interested in what he got out of the act. But now, as he watched Mia surrender to her own need, Jack recognized the emotional connection that could come along with sex.

She was completely vulnerable, trusting him to provide what she sought. And when Mia cried out and spasms shook her body again, he knew this wasn't just about physical satisfaction. They'd shared something deeper and more intense, something that now bound them together. With one last thrust, he joined her, gripping her hips as his orgasm overwhelmed him.

After it was over, they lay side by side, limbs still entwined, heartbeats growing slower. Jack pressed his forehead to hers, searching for the words to express how he felt. He felt exhilarated but sober, confused yet clear-headed, content yet strangely unsettled.

"Someday, Mia, I'm going to tell you that I love you. And I want you to think back to this moment."

"Why?"

"Because this was the time I wanted to say it first, but I didn't have the courage."

Mia reached up and smoothed her hand over his beard-roughened cheek. "I will," she murmured. "I'll remember every little detail." She snuggled into his body. "What do you think is going to happen tomorrow? Will they offer you a job?"

"I don't know. I made a couple of appearances on the network last year and they really liked my analysis of the post-season schedule. They even talked about giving me my own show, at some point."

"Really? I could watch you on television?"

"Yeah, if they still have the same thing in mind for me. I'll be on every night during the baseball season."

"Aren't you going to miss Chicago?" Mia asked.

"I think I need to move on," Jack said. "I've been stuck there a long time."

"What about your mom?"

Jack turned to face Mia. "I think that she'll be fine on her own. Maybe she'll meet someone new. And fall in love again. But it's her life to live."

Jack was determined not to let any more opportunities pass him by. He had a chance to build something wonderful with Mia and he planned to devote himself entirely to their future. He now realized just how strong his mother really was. It had been a surprise, but a very pleasant one.

A comfortable silence descended over them and Jack closed his eyes. Suddenly, his stomach growled and he rubbed it. "Ouch. I'm hungry."

"It's all that blood pumping through your body," she said. "Orgasms are good for you. Very healthy. They burn a lot of calories. I read that in some magazine."

Jack chuckled. "Good to know. Next time I catch a cold, I'll have to give you a call."

Jack pulled her leg over his hip, drawing her closer. "I'd be happy to help."

Her naked body fit so perfectly against his, as if she were made especially for him. Jack brushed the thought aside. He wasn't ready to make something out of this just yet.

"I have to tell you, I prefer this to dancing," Jack said. "It's much nicer without the clothes."

Mia sighed softly, then shrugged. "I never do things like this. I'm not an impetuous person. I'm like your mother. Every decision I make, I think about for days and days. But, with you... it just seemed like the right thing to do."

"Even though your father doesn't approve?"

"My father doesn't run my life," she said. "I've been preoccupied with family matters for too long. I need to start thinking about myself from now on."

"Well, maybe that's what we need to do. Stop thinking about them and start thinking about us."

"I like that there's an 'us' now," Mia murmured.

"Yeah, I think there is," Jack said. "As strange as it is, maybe we were the ones who were supposed to meet."

"You think?"

The sound of a cell phone broke the silence of the room. Jack rolled over and grabbed his BlackBerry. "Jack Quinn."

The production assistant on the other end of the line went through his itinerary with him for the following day, then asked if he needed anything.

"Maybe a suggestion for dinner," Jack said. "Something casual yet romantic?"

Mia laughed softly and then pushed up to press a kiss to his cheek.

The production assistant told him they'd make arrangements for dinner and send a car at seven. After he hung up, Jack sank back into the down pillows and pulled Mia close. "I'm really beginning to like California."

TWO DAYS LATER, Mia kicked off her shoes and walked into the kitchen of her father's house. She paused as she picked up the teakettle from on top of the stove, then glanced around. Even after she got her condo, she considered the house in Ross to be home. But all that had changed since Jack had come into her life. Wherever they spent time together now felt like home to her.

She'd left Jack in L.A. earlier that morning. He'd had his first round of interviews yesterday and they'd decided to keep him for another day. Rather than spend the day wandering around L.A. by herself, Mia had decided to fly back and see if she could straighten things out with her father.

She filled the teakettle and dropped it onto the stove, then went off in search of her dad. She found him sitting on the terrace, his late-afternoon cocktail in his hand. Mia glanced at her watch. It wasn't even 2:00 p.m. yet.

She opened the screen door and stepped outside. Her father turned at the sound and Mia was happy to see a smile on his face. "Hi, Daddy."

"Hello, Mimi."

She sat down at the table and folded her hands in front of her. "It's a little early for cocktail hour, isn't it?"

"Oh, I don't know. I don't think it really matters one way or the other, do you?" He stared at her for a long moment, then shook his head. "I'm sorry, Mimi. I really messed things up. I tried to—"

"Daddy, it's all right. I know why you said what you did. And you were right to be concerned for me. But I'm perfectly fine."

"Did Jack Quinn go home?"

"No," Mia said. "He might be staying a little longer. Maybe even relocating."

"I think I made a terrible mistake there, too," Ben said. "I said some things I wish I could take back."

"To Elyse?"

Ben nodded. "Your mother and I were always in such agreement. We never argued. It was like we had one mind. It wasn't that way with Elyse."

"Daddy, you can't disparage her son and expect her to smile and nod. You know how close they are and what they went through. Besides, you don't even know Jack. He's a great guy."

"He seduced my youngest daughter," Ben said.

"Actually, I seduced him. Or propositioned him."

"He didn't have to accept," Ben said.

"Oh, yes, he did. I wasn't about to give up. So you really can't blame everything on him. As for Elyse, she's pretty wonderful, too. You missed the boat on that one."

"Dating is hard," Ben said. "I'm way out of practice and I'm not even sure what the rules are these days."

"Come on," Mia said. "Let's get a cup of tea and I'll explain everything to you."

She took her father's cocktail away and he followed her into the kitchen, then took a seat at the breakfast bar. Over the next hour, they talked about everything, about her father's relationship with her mother, about his joy at reconnecting with Elyse and about his stubborn refusal to accept Mia's relationship with Jack.

In the end, Ben didn't really have any answers, but he knew that he'd made some mistakes. Mia poured herself another cup of tea and leaned over the counter, bracing her arms on the granite.

"So, what are you going to do now, Daddy?"

"I suppose I ought to apologize to Jack the first chance I get. Especially if he's going to be my son-in-law."

"I don't think that's been decided yet," Mia said. "Maybe you ought to apologize to him because he's a nice guy and your daughter likes him?"

"All right. First opportunity I get, that will happen."

"And what about Elyse?" she asked.

Her dad shook his head. "I think that's best left as is. There are so many complications, so many choices we'd each need to make. I think I got carried away with what I was feeling and I thought I could answer all those questions with one big, romantic gesture. But I figured out that we need to find some answers first." He took a sip of his tea. "So, Mimi, do you know what you're going to do now?"

"No," she said with a smile.

"I know you've put your personal life on hold these last few years. And when your mother was sick, you spent every spare minute with her. I know how much you've missed out on. I just wanted to make sure you weren't hurt."

"Daddy, that's the risk you take with falling in love. If there were guarantees with every relationship, everyone would live happily ever after."

Mia paused. "I like Elyse. I think Mom would have liked her, too."

"She's very opinionated."

"Elyse is used to taking care of herself. She's had to make all the decisions on her own."

"I could give her a good life," Ben said. "I'm financially secure and it seems that she's spent her whole life worrying about money. Even now, she watches every penny. I know how hard it is for her, but I want to make her life easier."

"Then you should. You worked hard for everything you have. You made all those choices." Mia picked up her mug and set it in the sink. "Daddy, if you want her back, I think you might have to fly to Chicago and convince her. Make one of those grand gestures again."

"Maybe I'm just too set in my ways to change. If I never remarry, I'll be fine. I have my work and my girls. And my grandchildren. That's enough to make me happy."

Mia poured Ben another mug of tea, straining the dry leaves through a sieve. Then she grabbed the milk from the fridge and put the perfect amount into her Dad's cup. Someday, maybe Elyse would know exactly how he liked his tea. Maybe she'd watch over him and tell the dry cleaners how he liked his shirts. Maybe she'd pack for his business trips and drive him to the airport.

She bent close and gave her dad a kiss on the cheek. "I need to get back," she said. "I've got to meet Jack later this evening."

She grabbed her keys from the counter. "And no more cocktails before four p.m.," Mia warned.

"Daddy! Daddy?"

A high-pitched voice cut through the silence of the house and Mia groaned inwardly as she recognized her sister Dani's voice. "In here," Mia called.

A moment later, her oldest sister burst through the door, her expensive luggage in tow. "You!" she said, pointing at Mia. "I've been calling you and calling you. Where have you been? Why haven't you picked up?" She spun on her father. "And you! I have to hear through friends that you're engaged?"

"He's not engaged," Mia said.

"I'm not engaged," Ben said.

"Daddy, you have to reconsider. I know you've been lonely lately, so I've decided that I'm going to spend more time here with you. I'll bring the kids and we'll have nice long weekends together. Of course, I'll have to bring the dog, too. David would never let me leave him at home, he'd tear the place apart. Now, it's time to put an end to this silliness. You are not engaged!"

"He's not engaged," Mia said.

"Not engaged," Ben said.

Dani looked back and forth between the two of them, frowning. "You're not?"

"No," Ben said.

A self-satisfied smile broke across her face. "Well, then. That's better. I'm glad you're both seeing my point of view."

"Daddy, I'll call you soon," she said, giving her dad a peck on the cheek. "Dani, have a cup of tea and relax."

Dani blinked in surprise. "You're leaving already?"

"Mimi has a boyfriend," Ben said with a sly smile. "His name is Jack."

"What? Why was I not informed of these things? Why doesn't anyone call me anymore?"

Mia hurried out of the house, giggling to herself. Yes, she had a boyfriend. A wonderful, handsome, sexy boyfriend. A tiny shiver skittered through her.

Jack was flying back into town that night. "I think I'm going to make my boyfriend a special dinner," she said to herself. Although she'd make sure that eating would be the last thing he'd have on his mind.

## 8

By the time Jack stepped out of the cab in front of Mia's flat, he was thoroughly exhausted. Not the pleasant kind of exhausted that he experienced after a long night in bed with Mia. This was the mind-numbing, frustration-inducing tired that made him want to crawl into bed and pull the covers over his head.

He'd gone to L.A. with such high hopes, certain that he could just pick up negotiations where he'd left off a year ago. But things at SportsNet had changed. Budgets had been cut and most of the money was going to well-established shows with hosts that had a fan base already. They weren't as enthusiastic about Jack's ability to build an audience as they had been last year.

He wasn't sure what he was going to tell Mia. Everything hinged on him moving out to L.A.

If he didn't find work in California, then that might be the end of their relationship.

Hell, he wouldn't blame her if she did bail. It was hard enough to make a romance work when the participants were living in the same town. But when they were living half a country apart, chances of success diminished exponentially.

Jack paid the cab driver, then turned to walk up the front steps. But he paused before he pressed the security buzzer to her flat. He could always take his chances and look for work somewhere else. Though he was a lifelong Cubs fan, he could switch loyalties to the Giants and write a column for the Examiner. Just across the Bay, Oakland had the A's and Los Angeles had two major league baseball teams. He was in a baseball rich environment.

Maybe he could tell her the negotiations for the job were ongoing. Then he could look for other work and hope that something came through before he ran out of cash. But he'd made a promise not to lie to Mia. They'd been together less than a week and he was already breaking the rules.

No, he'd tell her the truth. He'd lay out all his options and discuss them with her. Drawing a deep breath, he pushed the button. A moment later, the door swung open and Mia threw herself into his arms.

"You're home," she cried.

"I'm home," Jack said.

Funny how, after such a short time with her, this felt like home. Mia was here and she was all he needed to feel complete. He'd wondered at her father's capacity to fall in love so quickly, but Jack knew the feeling. At this moment in time, Jack Quinn's life was perfect.

"Come on," Mia said. "I have a surprise for you."

"Oh, sweetheart, I don't need any more surprises. You are the only thing I've been looking forward to seeing since I got on that plane."

When they reached the third floor landing, she opened the apartment door. Jack stepped inside to find the interior lit only by candles. The table was set for a fancy dinner and the smells wafting in from the kitchen caused his stomach to growl.

She'd made a celebration, Jack mused. Unfortunately, they weren't going to have anything to celebrate. Maybe this was one of those times when lying to Mia was the appropriate choice. How could he spoil her surprise with bad news?

"Wow, this is great," he said.

She took his hands and pulled him inside. Jack set his bag down next to the door and followed her. But the moment she stopped, he cupped her face between his hands and pulled her into a long, desperate kiss.

It was as simple as that, he thought. Every problem in the world could be solved by just kissing her. She gave him a strength that he didn't have on his own, a confidence that he needed to move forward. Jack ran his hands from her shoulders to her breasts to her hips and back again, reassuring himself that she really was back in his arms.

The instinct to connect, to test the limits of their desires was undeniable. Mia placed her palm on his chest, and drew back. "I bought champagne. Why don't I pour a couple glasses and you can tell me everything."

"That sounds nice," he murmured.

"Sit," she said, pointing to the sofa.

Jack slipped out of his jacket and tossed it over a nearby chair, then sank into Mia's overstuffed couch. He tipped his head back and closed his eyes, hoping to clear the chaos from his head.

"Here you go," she said, sitting down beside him.

He took the champagne flute from her hand and waited for her to settle. "Before we make a little toast here, I just want to tell you that I'm glad to be back here with you. I missed you after you left. And it's pretty clear to me that I'm not going to be happy unless we're together."

Mia smiled, then leaned close and brushed a kiss across his lips. "I feel the same way. I don't like being apart from you, either."

"So, I think we should toast to this, to the feeling that we were meant to be together, no matter what."

Mia held up her glass. "No matter what." She took a sip of her champagne. "So tell me what happened. When do you start? Are they going to cover relocation costs?"

"Things aren't going to happen quite as fast as we'd hoped," Jack said. "They're not looking to produce any new shows right now. They're interested in me, but they don't have the budget."

"What does that mean?" Mia asked, searching his gaze.

"It means that if I want to do a show for them, I'd have to find an independent production company to back me. Then they'd sell the show to the network, or to another sports network."

"Can you do that?"

"I don't know, Mia. I'd have to move out here without any promise of work and I'd have to find a television agent. We'd need to put together a whole package before trying to get backing."

He saw the disappointment in her eyes. But she quickly hid it behind a smile. "What are you going to do?"

"I'm going to find another job. And I'm going

to start looking in San Francisco. You've got two major league teams nearby. I can become a Giants fan."

"There are plenty of things you can do," Mia said. "And you can live here while you look. There's no reason for you to have your own place."

"Are you really sure you want to do that, Mia? I think I should keep my job in Chicago until I have something good lined up here."

"But then you'll need to go back home," Mia said.

"I'm going to need to go back home, anyway. But I think it would be great if you came with me. You could meet my sisters and I could show you around town."

"I have to go back to work next week," she said. "In fact, I was thinking of going into the office tomorrow to catch up." She pressed her face into his shoulder. "Tell me this is going to work out," she murmured.

Jack set his champagne down on the coffee table and drew her into his embrace. "It will. I promise. I don't want to let this go, Mia. I want to see how far it will take us."

She looked up at him. "Me, too."

Jack smiled. He needed to feel close to her now, to reassure himself that the connection between them hadn't been weakened.

Jack reached out and tangled his fingers in her hair, then turned her face up to meet his kiss. As the kiss deepened, he felt his reaction, deep at the core of his being.

Taking her hand, Jack pulled her along to the bedroom, their lips still tasting, tongues still teasing. They fell onto the neatly made bed, Jack yanking her down on top of him. He pulled the shoulder of her dress down, exposing her chest and neck and trailed a line of kisses along her collarbone. But when he could go no farther, she sat up and let her arms drop out of the sleeves. The bodice of the dress fell to her waist and a long breath escaped his lips.

Jack continued his exploration and when he reached her breast, he circled her nipple with his tongue then gently drew it into his mouth. The pleasure was too much to bear and Mia cried out, holding him close as desire pulsed through her body.

"I don't want to live without you," he murmured. Jack rolled her onto her back, then moved to her other breast. Her fingers furrowed through his hair and he molded his mouth to her flesh.

"Yes," she replied, breathlessly. "Oh, yes."

"How much longer do I have to wait to take your clothes off?" he asked.

"Now would be fine," she replied.

But as he reached for the buttons on the front

of her dress, the ring on Jack's cell phone stopped him. He groaned and reached for his pocket. He thought it might be the producers from SportsNet, but he saw his mother's name come up on the screen.

Jack showed the screen to Mia. "Answer it," she said.

"Hi, Mom. What's up?"

"I have the most wonderful news! I've just been contacted by an attorney," she said. "He told me that we have an inheritance coming from some distant relative in Ireland. He wants to meet with me tomorrow at the house."

Jack's instincts instantly went on alert. "Mom, don't you dare let a stranger into the house. This sounds like some kind of scam to get you to open the door."

"He knows my address," she said.

"You told him?"

"No, he said his investigator has been looking for me. Actually, he already knew my address. And he knew all about your father. He seemed like a very nice man, Jack. I think there might be something to this."

"Mom, I want you to pack a bag and go stay with a friend tonight. I'm going to call the Chicago P.D. and let them know. Promise me you'll leave tonight."

"You know, he told me the name of our rela-

tive. Aileen Quinn. She's a famous author, Jack.
I looked her up on my computer. She's sold millions of books."

"Mom, I'm going to fly out tomorrow. I'll be
home before you know it and we'll take care of
this. Promise me you're going to leave the house
right after you hang up. Drive out to Barrington
and stay with Katie. I'm going to call her right
now and tell her to expect you."

"All right. I'll go. But I really think you need
to talk to this man. He says you're going to receive an inheritance, as well."

By the time Jack hung up, he was more than
a little worried. His mother was a very smart
woman, but she tended to see the best in people.
She was far too trusting. Her trip to California
to see Ben McMahon was a perfect example.
And now this.

Jack tossed the phone aside and cursed softly.
"I'm going to have to take a trip back to Chicago
tomorrow," he said. "My mom has herself mixed
up in some kind of scam."

"I understand," Mia said, curling up beside
him. "You're going to come back, aren't you?"

"As soon as I can," Jack promised. "It will
only be a few days. A week at the most."

TEN DAYS LATER, JACK SAT alone with his mother
in the attorney's office. He glanced over at his

mother, then looked back down at the paper he was supposed to sign. "I still don't believe this. I keep waiting for the camera to come out and tell me I've been punked."

"Punked?"

"You know," Jack said. "Fooled. Suckered. This is one of those deals that looks too good to be true."

"Stop," Elyse said. "Don't insult the man. He's giving us a gift and you're being ungrateful."

The man that his mother was supposed to meet with, the man she'd run away from the week before, turned out to be a Chicago attorney, hired by a representative of the Irish author Aileen Quinn. After a thorough vetting of his credentials and a few calls to his friends in the legal profession, Jack was forced to admit that the boogeyman he'd created was really a white knight. Bestselling author Aileen Quinn had set out to find the descendants of her four brothers, hoping to gift them with a small portion of her formidable estate. The Quinn family of Chicago—Elyse, Jack and his two younger sisters, Katie and Kris, would each receive a half-million dollars. And if that wasn't enough, they'd receive more once they paid a visit to their great aunt. Elyse had already made her travel plans, even before she got the inheritance. But

Jack still wasn't sure he wanted to believe his good fortune.

Throughout his childhood, it seemed as if luck had always eluded his family. It had been a constant struggle to keep the lights turned on and the cable bill paid, to have enough for food and decent clothes and school supplies. There had never been anything extra—until now.

Jack looked over at his mom. "Can you believe this?"

Her eyes were shining. More than anything, he knew what this inheritance meant to his mother. She could enjoy her retirement now, secure in the fact that she'd have enough to keep her house and pay her taxes and travel whenever she wanted to.

Since he'd been back, he and his mother had talked about the inheritance any number of times. But the subject of Ben McMahon hadn't come up once. He'd once thought that Elyse might have found financial security with a guy like Ben, but now she had that all on her own. Perhaps everything turned out the way it was supposed to.

When the lawyer entered the room, Jack asked, "Can you explain to me again how this works?"

"It's quite simple. You sign the paperwork and I give you a check," the attorney said.

"No, I mean, how are we related to Aileen Quinn?"

Elyse put her papers down. "I can answer that. Aileen Quinn had four older brothers. The family was split up when she was just a baby. Her brother Conal ended up here in Chicago. He was your grandfather. I never met him, but your grandmother was at our wedding. She died when you were three. They had two children, your father and his sister, Mary Katherine, who became a nun and now lives somewhere in Central America. After your father died, we lost touch."

"We have one relative and she just happens to be ridiculously wealthy," Jack murmured. "Who'd have thought?"

He picked up the pen and signed the papers, then pushed them across the conference room table to the attorney. After he notarized the signature, he handed Jack an envelope. Holding his breath, Jack peeked inside to see a check with more zeros than he'd ever seen in his life.

It was like he'd won the lottery. He was now financially secure enough to do whatever he wanted with his life. He could take time off work and write a book. He could produce his own show for a sports network. He could lease a private jet to fly back and forth to San Francisco every weekend.

Jack sat back in his chair and smiled. He

hadn't told Mia about his windfall. Until a few days ago, he wasn't sure it was real. But now, with the check in his hand, Jack had to admit, being well-off felt good.

When they finished with the lawyer, Jack and Elyse said goodbye to the lawyer. He was scheduled to meet with Katie and Kris later in the week and had encouraged them all to make plans to visit Aileen in Ireland.

Jack walked with his mother out to the elevator and they stepped inside. "I think I'm going to buy you lunch," he said. "Any place you want. Cost is no concern."

Elyse laughed. "I couldn't help but think of your father, how happy this would have made him. He was always so proud of his Irish heritage. It's almost like it's a gift from him, too, don't you think?"

Jack nodded. "What are you going to do now, Mom? This money gives you a lot of freedom. A lot of choices."

"I haven't decided yet," she said softly. "Since I got back from California, I've kind of found myself at a crossroads. Spending time out there made me realize that I'd like to have a companion, a man who I could spend time with. I wouldn't have to get married, but it would be nice to have an occasional date."

"I think that would be a great idea," Jack said. "Any prospects?"

"Ben has been emailing me," she said. "He apologized for his behavior and asked if we could Skype this weekend."

Jack shook his head. "I should have never taught you how to use social media."

"You can't put that toothpaste back into the tube," she teased. "I just set up a Twitter account."

"Are you going to see him again?" Jack asked.

"Are you and Mia going to see each other again?"

"Yes," Jack said. "I'm flying back there this weekend."

"Then, I think Ben and I would be better off as friends. And someday, parents of the bride and groom?"

"We're not there yet," Jack said.

When they reached the lobby, Jack stepped out of the elevator and held out his arm for his mother. But Elyse pointed across the street at a bookstore. "I need to pick up something," she said.

They hurried against the light and when they got inside, he followed his mother to the fiction department. She walked along the shelves, then stopped and pulled out a paperback. "What are you looking for?" Jack asked.

She found a book and took it off the shelf. "Aileen Quinn."

"Wow," Jack said, taking the book from her. "I guess she is real."

His mother grabbed several other novels from the same section. "I think I'm going to skip lunch today and spend some time reading. I've got a trip to Ireland to get ready for."

"All right," he said. "But don't spend all that money in one place. And be careful on the train."

Jack headed back out to the street. There was one thing he did need to do, one last step he had to take. The offices for the Tribune were only a few blocks away and the weather was warm and sunny, a perfect May day in Chicago.

This had been his town, the heartbeat of his life. It was hard to imagine loving any place as much as he loved his city on the lake. But once he moved to California, Chicago would be nothing more than a destination for an occasional trip home.

When he got to the office, he walked through the maze of cubicles toward the sports editor's office. As usual, Jim Mortonsen was buried in work. His desk was stacked with books and DVDs, intermingled with papers and old coffee cups.

"Hey, boss. You have a few minutes?"

"I'm glad you're here," Jim said. "I've got something I need to talk to you about."

"Same here," Jack said. "Maybe I should go first."

"No, you're going to want to hear this." Jim pointed to a chair. "Sit."

Jack grabbed a stack of newspapers on the chair and set them on the floor, then sat down.

"I'm sure you know that the Tribune syndicates a number of our columnists. And with the state of the newspaper industry lately, the guys in the head office are looking for more opportunities to syndicate our best writers. But that means a change in editorial direction, a more national direction. They want you on the list, Jack."

"They want to syndicate my column?"

"Not the column as it is now. They want you to focus more on baseball as a sport and not specifically the Cubs. You'll get your own website linked to ours. You'll develop a national audience." He paused. "I know you've been looking at that job out at SportsNet," he said. "I also know you interviewed out there this week. We don't want to lose you, Jack. If you're interested, then we're willing to pursue this."

"Would I have to stay in Chicago?"

Jim shrugged. "I don't know. I can't see why you would. You'd travel during the season, maybe write a book during the off season. If I had your writing talents, I'd jump at this. Forget SportsNet."

"Tell them I'm interested," Jack said. "I'll be happy to sit down and talk to them."

As he strode back through the newsroom a few minutes later, Jack couldn't help but smile. When things were going bad, they were bad. But he'd never experienced a run of good luck like this. First, meeting Mia. Then the inheritance. And now, a job offer that could solve all his problems.

Jack's cell phone rang and he looked down at the screen to see a text from Mia. He smiled to himself and pressed the button to read the message. But as he did, his smile faded.

*I can't do this any longer. It's over.*

MIA STARED DOWN AT HER cell phone. She'd sent the message yesterday and Jack hadn't responded. What did that mean? she wondered.

She wanted to take the text back, to erase it from her memory and his. But she couldn't. Once it had left her phone, it was out of her control.

"Stupid girl," she murmured.

Since Jack had left last week, she'd been feeling more and more insecure. She'd begun to question her own feelings, wondering if everything that she'd believed was real was just all part of some silly infatuation.

Maybe she wasn't meant to be in a relationship. Absence was supposed to make the heart grow fonder. It only made her crazy with doubts and insecurities. Though Jack had called her at least two or three times a day, Mia found herself wondering if he was beginning to question his own feelings, as well.

Was that why he was so reluctant to return to San Francisco? She kept asking when he was coming back and for the past three or four days, he'd given her vague answers.

Maybe this was all in her imagination. Maybe she was just blowing up the situation in her head. Sending the text yesterday was more of a provocation than anything else. But he hadn't responded. Now what was she supposed to do?

Jack had promised to always tell her the truth. So if he wasn't interested in returning, then he would have told her. But he also should have responded to her text.

Mia looked both ways, then crossed the street and began the long hike up the hill to her flat. Even a rush of work couldn't distract her thoughts. She had two big design projects that had come in on Monday and needed a quick turnaround.

Mia slowed her pace as she came to the steepest part of the hill. She usually drove to work, but a new exercise regime had become part of her plan to forget about Jack Quinn. She'd walk the two miles to and from work every day. She'd also decided to give up caffeine and eat at least three servings of vegetables a day.

As she approached her flat, she saw a figure sitting on the front steps. Her heart leaped as she thought it might be Jack. But then she chided herself for even going there. Her neighbor often sat outside on the stoop on sunny afternoons, doing his crossword puzzle and sipping a latte from the nearby coffee shop.

It wasn't until she was almost home that Mia realized she had been right all along. She hesitated as she saw Jack push to his feet. He'd only been gone a week, but it had seemed like much longer.

A tiny gasp slipped from her lips as their gazes met and in that instant, she knew how wrong she'd been to doubt him. It was all there in his eyes—the need, the passion, the affection.

Mia slowly approached him, wondering who would be the first to speak. But in the end, she just walked right into his arms and pressed her forehead to his chest. Jack groaned softly and pulled her tight against his body, his hand tangling in her hair.

They stood on the sidewalk for a long time,

silent, the simple contact enough to convey their feelings. And when she finally drew back, Jack captured her face in his hands and pulled her into a long, desperate kiss.

"Don't ever do that to me again," he murmured, his lips skimming over her eyes and nose before he found her mouth again.

"I'm sorry," Mia said. "I'm so, so sorry."

"I thought I'd lost you."

"It was stupid. I was just feeling insecure."

"Mia, you don't have to feel that way with me. I know what I want and all I want is you." He kissed her again, this time more gently, as if his own worries had been calmed.

"It just all happened so fast," Mia said. "And I kept thinking that I'd imagined it all. How does anyone fall in love in just four days? That's crazy!"

Jack chuckled. "No, not crazy. We're just… efficient."

"There's nothing wrong with being efficient," Mia said. "I'm so glad you came back."

"I had to. I have big news. Very big news. I didn't want to tell you until I was sure what was going to happen, but you are looking at a man with his future in his own hands."

"Did SportsNet call?"

Jack shook his head. "Fate did. I just inherited a boatload of money from a long-lost relative in

Ireland. Enough to make it possible to choose a new life for myself. I also got an offer to write a nationally syndicated column about baseball. So, my prospects are looking up."

"I've always wanted a guy with prospects," she said.

"You have one. And now, you're going to have to figure out how long you want to keep him."

"Would forever be long enough?" Mia asked.

"I think forever would be just about right." With a laugh, Jack pulled her into his arms, then scooped her up and carried her up the front steps. "You know, I might be moving in for a while. Just until I get things settled. Can you handle a roommate?"

"Well, there will be few rules," Mia said.

"Oh, the rules. Isn't that where we started?" Jack asked.

"These will be much easier to follow. First, you have to tell me that you love me every single day, rain or shine."

"I love you," Jack said. "I'm pretty sure I loved you the first moment I saw you."

"And you have to kiss me at least once every hour when we're together. It doesn't have to be a huge kiss, but it needs to be regular."

"Have I filled my quota for the day?"

"Not quite, but we'll get to that in a bit."

"And finally, you have to make love to me every night from now until forever."

"What about mornings?"

"Those would be optional," Mia said. "But encouraged. Do you think you can follow those rules?"

"Absolutely," Jack said.

They got to the landing and Mia unlocked the door to her flat, letting them both inside. As soon as the door was closed behind them, he pulled her into his arms again and enjoyed a long, lazy kiss, his mouth teasing at hers until she was forced to surrender.

It was all so perfect that it was difficult to believe it was real. But then Jack scooped her up and carried her into the bedroom and she knew the best was about to come.

"What are you doing?" Mia asked.

Jack tossed her down on the bed. "Rule number three. Make love to you at least once a day. I figured I better get started right away. Why delay when I'm perfectly ready to take on my duties right this moment?"

Mia giggled, then got to her knees. She quickly stripped off her blouse. "All right. I think I'm ready for the rest of our life to begin."

They both fell back onto the bed, laughing and teasing as they worked their way out of the last of their clothes. Mia had never really believed that she would find true love. For her, it had always proved elusive. But then Jack walked into her life and changed everything.

Perhaps it was luck. Maybe it was fate. Or maybe they'd just been waiting for each other all that time. But Mia wasn't ever going to doubt their feelings again. She'd found forever in his arms and that's exactly where she intended to stay. Forever.

# 9

"WE'RE GOING TO BE LATE," Jack said. "All the guests will be waiting on us."

Mia laughed as she tugged off his tie, then tossed it aside. They'd dressed once already and now they'd just have to do it again. "We have plenty of time. The ceremony isn't scheduled to start for another twenty minutes. Nobody will start looking for us for at least another ten. I'm sure you can wrap everything up by then."

Jack cursed softly. "You know, we're going to have to have a little discussion about these rules that you keep setting down. Sometimes, I get the feeling that you enjoy enforcing them a little too much."

"Really?" Mia asked. She reached for the zipper of her gown and slowly drew it down. She tossed it over a chair and stood there, wearing only a sexy bustier and lacy panties. The moment Jack got a look at the underwear, he shook his head.

"Nice. Now you've taken to cheating."

"How is sexy underwear cheating?"

"You know I can't resist that stuff." He stepped forward and began to work at the laces but Mia shook her head. "We're not going to have time for that now," she said. "Not unless you want to be late."

Jack pulled her down on the bed, then sat up, bracing his hands behind him. "God, you are so beautiful. Just perfect."

Mia had never believed she was anything out of the ordinary. But now, with Jack looking at her, his eyes glazed with desire, she could believe it. Mia pulled him to his feet and slowly began to take his clothes off. He stood silently watching her. With each piece of clothing she discarded, Mia took to the time to appreciate the body beneath.

Everything about him was exactly what she found beautiful in a man. His broad chest and sharply defined shoulders, his narrow waist, his long, muscular legs. He wore his masculinity with such a careless grace, as if he barely thought about the impression he made.

She pressed a kiss to his chest and then slowly worked her way over to his nipple. He drew a sharp breath as her tongue teased it to a stiff peak before moving on to the opposite side.

Though they only had a few minutes to spare, Mia wasn't in any hurry to move things along. She knew him so well that she could predict his reactions to her touch, to her caresses. This might be the only chance they had all day to be together and she was going to take complete advantage of it.

Slowly, she moved against him, around him, always keeping contact with his skin, her fingertips skimming his flesh as she moved. When she was behind him, Mia reached around and ran her palm along the length of his stiff shaft.

Jack groaned as he slipped his hand around her waist and pulled their bodies together. His cock pressed against her stomach, the hard ridge meeting the lacy fabric of her bustier. And when she reached down to caress him, Mia heard him suck in a sharp breath and then groan softly as her fingers closed around him.

She loved the effect her touch had on his body, the way she could control him with just a movement. She nuzzled her face into his chest and then slowly moved lower, leaving a damp trail with her lips and tongue.

When she reached his belly, he tangled his fingers in her hair, trying to slow her descent. But Mia was determined to test the limits of her seductive skills. She'd never felt bolder or more empowered than she did now. She wasn't just playing at sex, she was experiencing it, fully and completely with a man she loved.

When she took him into her mouth, his reaction was swift. His body jerked and he clutched at her hair, a tremor running through him. Mia was gentle at first, using her tongue to tease at him. But then, as his passion began to build, she showed him how much she was willing to give him.

Again and again, he drew her back and she knew he was fighting for control. But then, she'd edge him even closer the next time. It was like a game they played, Mia in control and Jack fighting her all the way.

Time seemed to stand still for them. They were existing in a haze of need where every sense was heightened. When he touched her body, shivers skittered over her skin, and when he whispered her name, it sounded like music to her ears.

She tried to think rationally, but there was no reality anymore, just this crazy fantasy with this man she adored. When she'd teased him long enough she slowly kissed her way back to his mouth.

"Are you ready?" she whispered.

"We should probably use a condom," he murmured. "Just to keep things tidy."

Mia bent down and retrieved her clutch purse from the floor and opened it, pulling out a length of three. "I always come prepared," she said.

"You expected this to happen? Here? Today?"

"Darling, when it comes to you, I know to expect the unexpected. And you have to admit, this is pretty unexpected."

"I guess there are all kinds of surprises to come."

They finished quickly, then dressed and hurried out of Mia's bedroom. By the time they got downstairs, the entire family was already assembled in the garden of her father's house, standing in a semicircle and watching the doors expectantly.

"Where were you?" Dani whispered.

"I was having trouble with my zipper," Mia said with a smile.

She heard Jack laugh and she turned to him, pressing her finger to her lips. "They're coming."

A moment later, the sound of a solo guitar filled the late summer air. The French doors opened and Elyse stepped out, dressed in a vintage gown, looking like a 1950's movie star. She wore an orchid in her hair and carried a bouquet of the same.

She was joined by Mia's father and they

slowly walked toward the group, their children and grandchildren assembled before them. Mia had promised herself she wouldn't cry, but in the end, she couldn't help herself. Jack slipped his arm around her and pulled her close, kissing the top of her head.

"Someday that's going to be us," he whispered.

Mia nodded. "Soon," she said.

"But we're not going to follow your rules that day. The sex is going to have to wait until after the ceremony."

Mia smiled through her tears. "I suppose that's something we could negotiate."

"That, my dear, is a deal breaker."

Mia had no doubt she'd accept his terms. After all, she had decided to spend the rest of her life with him. A few compromises could be expected.

After all, forever was a very long time.

# Epilogue

AILEEN QUINN CLOSED her eyes and turned her face up to the warmth of the sun. She'd found a spot on the terrace away from the breeze coming off the ocean and had had the comfortable chaise moved to take advantage of it.

"Miss Quinn?"

She opened her eyes to find her housekeeper, Sally, peering at her with a concerned frown. "Yes?"

"Oh, dear, you gave me a start. You were lying so still I thought you were—"

Aileen giggled. "Did you think I was dead, Sally?" She shook her head. "After nearly ninety-seven years, my dear, I know the end is probably just around the corner. But I can assure you that it won't come until my business here is completely finished."

"Then I would suggest that you don't finish

writing a book until you've started a new one. Your work will never be done then."

"Oh, well done, Sally. Clever girl. I must remember to do that. But I was talking about family business."

"I swear that will kill you if anything does. Four children in this house at the same time. It's a miracle any one of us survived."

The granddaughters of Aileen's brother Conal had paid a visit the previous week. Katherine and Kristina Quinn had each brought along their two children and it had been a lively group, the two young mothers fascinated with their Irish heritage and their children fascinated with running about the countryside without their shoes.

Aileen had never been a mother, so she wasn't one to judge, but she did find the children a bit rowdy—but utterly charming.

The three boys and a girl had taken to calling her Granty Ailey and had started each day with a breakfast recitation of how well behaved they promised to be and ended each day with a dinner recitation of the trouble they'd managed to find in the course of the previous ten hours.

"Perhaps we ought to encourage your great-nieces and nephews to leave their children at home on future visits," Sally said.

"Don't be silly," Aileen said. "I want to know them all."

"Then I don't have to tell you that I'm glad Mr. Stephens hasn't paid a visit lately. Perhaps the tide of guests might stop for a bit."

The thought that she might leave this world without knowing the fate of her brothers Diarmuid and Lochlan had caused Aileen more than just a small bit of anxiety. Perhaps she'd been too optimistic. After all, Mr. Stephens was looking for boys who had left Ireland and disappeared into the vastness of the world.

Tomas had ended up in Australia while Conal had settled in the U.S., in the city of Chicago. Where would she find the other two? Where had the fates cast them?

"Mr. Stephens says he has a lead on Lochlan but I suspect that it's another dead end as he calls it," Aileen told Sally. "But I do have a plan of my own if he fails. I thought I just might put out the word to any Quinn descendant in the world to prove their connection to one of my brothers and they will be rewarded. But I've had cause to reconsider that plan."

"Good. You'd have every chancer and bowsie standing on our front step looking for some of your money to line their pockets. Best to leave this to the experts."

Aileen smiled and nodded. "Of course, you're right." She drew a deep breath and sighed. "I do think it's quite fortunate that I didn't discover all these relatives until late in my career. I might never have gotten any work done with all the reports and visits and such."

"Will you write today?" Sally asked. "You haven't done much on your autobiography."

"Oh, I think I'll just rest a bit today and start fresh tomorrow. Mr. Stephens did say that he has a promising new lead for Lochlan. In Nova Scotia of all places. I get the sense that Lochlan's descendants might not want to be found."

"Why is that?"

"I'm sure Mr. Stephens will ferret out the truth for us one way or another." Aileen smiled. "Now, why don't we have our tea in the sunshine today, Sally? This day is too perfect to waste indoors."

Aileen listened to the housekeeper's footsteps as they faded on the stone. She'd thought her life was coming to its last chapter. And then, she'd discovered the existence of a family—four brothers—four chances to claim a connection to someone who'd live on after she was gone.

She had no intention of finishing this book until every last one of them had been found. Only then would her life be complete.

\* \* \* \* \*

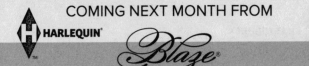
### #747 WAKING UP TO YOU • *Forbidden Fantasies*
by Leslie Kelly

When Candace Reid decides to marry her gay best friend, she gives herself permission to indulge in one last fling. Only, once she meets rugged Oliver McKean, she realizes that a night spent in his arms won't be nearly enough....

### #748 NORTHERN REBEL • *Uniformly Hot!*
by Jennifer LaBrecque

It doesn't take nurse Delphi Reynold long to see that Marine Lars Reinhardt is trouble. He's cocky, he's arrogant...and he's so hot, she can't keep her hands to herself! Then again, what's life without a little trouble?

### #749 MY DOUBLE LIFE
by Joanne Rock

Courtney Masterson has a secret. By day she's a financial researcher. By night she's an exotic dancer. Her two personae are totally separate—until Trey Fraser falls for both of them....

### #750 MIDNIGHT SPECIAL • *The Wrong Bed*
by Tawny Weber

Michael Hunter is a hot, rugged FBI agent. Marni Clare is a savvy, sexy reporter. Even though they are on opposite sides of a national case, they can't resist being on the same side of the bed....

---

SPECIAL EXCERPT FROM

HARLEQUIN®

*Blaze*®

Bestselling author Leslie Kelly brings you the
ultimate Forbidden Fantasy!

A promised woman. A sexy groundskeeper.
Lady Chatterley, look out!

Here's a sneak peek at

# *Waking Up To You*

Gently pushing her, Oliver ordered, "Go."

All because he needed *her* to be the one who walked away
and ended this before it really began? As if he had no free will?
As if unless she did, he wouldn't be able to stop himself from
doing to her exactly what she'd practically dared him to do?

*You don't want him to do it, either, remember? You know you
can't do this.*

No. She might want Oliver, and having sex with him might
even be worth what she would go through afterward if people
found out. But she needed to cool this, here and now. She had
to be the one who walked away.

Which still wasn't going to be easy.

"I'm telling you, you really don't want to watch me walking
up those stairs."

"Yes. I really do."

"You'll regret it."

"Hell, I already regret it," he said, tunneling both his hands
through his hair this time, leaving it more tousled than before.

HBEXP79751

"Not as much as you're about to."

Without another word, she spun around again, squared her shoulders, stiffened her spine and ascended the stairs. He stood below, watching her, and when she reached the fourth one, she couldn't help pausing to glance over her shoulder at him.

"Oh, Oliver, do you want to know why I didn't want to walk up the stairs until you left?"

He didn't reply, just gave her an inscrutable look.

She told him anyway. "Because of this."

Candace took another step, knowing she'd reached the point of no return. Knowing full well he could now see what she was *not* wearing beneath her robe.

She wished she could say his strangled, guttural cry of helpless frustration made her feel better about walking away from what she sensed could be the best sex of her life.

But she just couldn't.

**Pick up WAKING UP TO YOU by Leslie Kelly, available April 23 wherever you buy Harlequin Blaze books.**

**As a special treat to you, you will also find Leslie's classic story *Overexposed* in the same volume. That's 2 great books for 1 great price!**

# REQUEST YOUR FREE BOOKS!
## 2 FREE NOVELS PLUS 2 FREE GIFTS!

◊ HARLEQUIN®

*Blaze*®

### red-hot reads!

**YES!** Please send me 2 FREE Harlequin® Blaze™ novels and my 2 FREE gifts (gifts are worth about $10). After receiving them, if I don't wish to receive any more books, I can return the shipping statement marked "cancel." If I don't cancel, I will receive 4 brand-new novels every month and be billed just $4.49 per book in the U.S. or $4.96 per book in Canada. That's a savings of at least 14% off the cover price. It's quite a bargain. Shipping and handling is just 50¢ per book in the U.S. and 75¢ per book in Canada.* I understand that accepting the 2 free books and gifts places me under no obligation to buy anything. I can always return a shipment and cancel at any time. Even if I never buy another book, the two free books and gifts are mine to keep forever.

150/350 HDN FV42

| | |
|---|---|
| Name | (PLEASE PRINT) |

| | | |
|---|---|---|
| Address | | Apt. # |

| | | |
|---|---|---|
| City | State/Prov. | Zip/Postal Code |

Signature (if under 18, a parent or guardian must sign)

Mail to the **Harlequin® Reader Service:**
**IN U.S.A.:** P.O. Box 1867, Buffalo, NY 14240-1867
**IN CANADA:** P.O. Box 609, Fort Erie, Ontario L2A 5X3

**Want to try two free books from another line?**
**Call 1-800-873-8635 or visit www.ReaderService.com.**

\* Terms and prices subject to change without notice. Prices do not include applicable taxes. Sales tax applicable in N.Y. Canadian residents will be charged applicable taxes. Offer not valid in Quebec. This offer is limited to one order per household. Not valid for current subscribers to Harlequin Blaze books. All orders subject to credit approval. Credit or debit balances in a customer's account(s) may be offset by any other outstanding balance owed by or to the customer. Please allow 4 to 6 weeks for delivery. Offer available while quantities last.

**Your Privacy**—The Harlequin® Reader Service is committed to protecting your privacy. Our Privacy Policy is available online at www.ReaderService.com or upon request from the Harlequin Reader Service.

We make a portion of our mailing list available to reputable third parties that offer products we believe may interest you. If you prefer that we not exchange your name with third parties, or if you wish to clarify or modify your communication preferences, please visit us at www.ReaderService.com/consumerchoice or write to us at Harlequin Reader Service Preference Service, P.O. Box 9062, Buffalo, NY 14269. Include your complete name and address.

HBI3R